Fly: Goose Girl Retold

DEMELZA CARLTON

A tale in the Romance a Medieval Fairy Tale series

This is a work of fiction. Names, characters, businesses, places, events and incidents are either the products of the author's imagination or used in a fictitious manner. Any resemblance to actual persons, living or dead, or actual events is purely coincidental.

Copyright © 2017 Demelza Carlton

Lost Plot Press

All rights reserved.

ISBN-13: 978-1979865241

ISBN-10: 1979865248

DEDICATION

This one's for May, too…because her suggestion that I write this book opened the gate so Ava could fly.

One

"Hurry up, you goose! If the guard returns, you'll get us all into trouble!" Lagle hissed.

Ava bent to retrieve the towel she'd dropped, then, obedient to her sister's order, broke into a run as she fancied she heard footsteps. If the guards caught the princesses out of the harem, they'd only lock the girls back in, but then they wouldn't get to swim.

And Lagle would definitely blame her. The

guards might not punish princesses, but Lagle was the Queen's daughter, making her the highest ranking princess among the myriad daughters of minor wives and concubines, and she would be certain to make Ava's life hell.

So Bianca led the way to the pool, swearing she'd gotten directions from one of the young princes who'd watched soldiers learning to swim there. Lagle strode behind her with her proud head held high, and Ava brought up the rear with a bundle of towels that was too heavy for her to carry without dropping them along the way. When yet another towel slipped from her grasp, earning her a glare from Lagle, Ava was almost ready to give up and head back to the harem. The only thing that kept her putting one foot in front of the other was the thought of the tantalising coolness of immersing her whole body in water, while the rest of the palace sweltered in the unseasonable spring heat. To stop being sweaty and sticky for just a few hours would be bliss, and well worth the walk even with a load of towels.

And Bianca would be there, Ava consoled herself. The expedition might be Lagle's idea, but without Bianca, it could not have happened. Bianca was the only one of her sisters who seemed to see Ava at all. To the rest, she was invisible, a princess so low in the pecking order that they rarely remembered her name. Most of them didn't remember her mother's name, either, for Sumi had died giving birth to Ava, a scant seven months after entering the harem. A captured prize from one of the King's many battles, Ava had heard, who the King had favoured for a few short weeks until some other jewel of his harem caught his eye. A harem Ava had left only a handful of times, because the King protected his daughters fiercely, whether they were as highborn as Lagle or as insignificant as Ava.

If he knew three of them had sneaked out of the harem, heading for the soldiers' barracks…Ava shivered.

Moonlight sparkled on the pool surface, making it look almost magical. Two towels escaped from her arms, which made her deliberately drop the rest in a pile on the tiles. Bianca and Lagle had already started to shed their robes, so Ava shyly followed suit.

Bianca entered the water silently, slipping under the surface before swimming away from the edge. Ava was impressed, and she began to wonder how often Bianca had visited this pool before. She couldn't have learned such swimming skills in the harem.

Lagle jumped into the water with a splash and a squeal. Ava opened her mouth to beg her to be quieter, but she knew it was no use. When had Lagle ever listened to anyone, let alone Ava?

Ava crept across the tiles to the pool edge. The stone was surprisingly warm underfoot, perhaps from lying in the sun all day, and it was with considerable relief that she dipped her toes into the water. "It's cold!" she exclaimed.

"It's best to get in all at once. You'll soon grow used to it," Bianca advised.

Ava pulled her foot out of the water, and a breezy gust chilled her wet skin. If one foot could be this cold, what would it be like when she hoisted her whole body out of the water, soaking wet? Why, she would freeze.

"I've changed my mind," she murmured, backing away from the water.

Lagle sent a wave of water in her direction. "Coward! Swelter, then. See if I care."

Ava reached her clothes and struggled back into them. She couldn't be sure if she'd tied everything correctly, in the dark without a mirror and all, but she did the best she could.

She sat beside the towels, drowsing in the heat while her sisters splashed. None of them had slept well with the heat these last few nights, but her airless cubicle was flush against the western wall of the women's palace, turning it into a veritable oven. Perhaps if she lay here for a few moments until the other girls were finished in the water…

Ava stretched out on the towels and slipped into a dream.

Two

Not for the first time, Yun wondered when this nightmare would end. Certainly not today, or tomorrow, for there were too many corpses to bury after this latest battle. Not that he'd be doing it – burying the dead was work for common soldiers, not princes.

Princes were supposed to take pleasure in sights like this, or so his older brothers told him. Then again, his brothers took pleasure in a great many things that turned Yun's stomach.

Take Gang, the heir to the throne and their

illustrious general, and Chao, second in line on both counts. They had set up camp just outside of town, and the pen where their horses should have been was now filled with sobbing women. The wives and daughters of the men who had died on the battlefield, defending the village, Yun assumed from their clothing.

He didn't need to follow the grunts, whimpers and screams to know his brothers had already started celebrating their victory. He wished he didn't have to witness it, but their father would not wait.

Shoving his way into Gang's tent, he averted his eyes from his rutting brother and the girl who squirmed and sobbed beneath him.

"What word shall I send to Father about the battle?" Yun asked.

"Can't it wait?" Gang grunted. He backhanded the girl across the face. "Silence! I can't hear a thing over your whining!"

"I wish it could, but Father must know our losses, and how many – "

"Enough!" Gang roared, drawing his dagger. He plunged the blade into the girl's throat, then yanked it out again. While the girl choked on her own blood, he rose to his feet and tugged down his robe. "What did you say? I couldn't hear you over that bitch's complaints. I told her to shut her mouth, but like all women, she wouldn't listen. She would have made a terrible wife. I did the world a favour." He grinned, wiping his dagger on the dead girl's ripped garments before sheathing it at his waist.

Yun fought down the bile rising up in his throat. How he'd grown up in the same household with Gang, he did not know. "I said, Father will want to know how many of our men died, and how many of the enemy. We must send a rider today."

Gang shrugged. "I don't know. Ask Chao. He keeps track of such things. Can't you see I'm busy?" He ambled out to the pen and seized the nearest girl by her hair. When she screamed in pain, Gang drew his dagger and sliced off her tongue. Then he dragged the gurgling girl to his tent.

Judging by the screams coming from Chao's tent, Yun wouldn't like what he found there, either. But, unlike his brothers, he was an obedient son.

Yun was gratified to find Chao still had his clothes on, though he had a girl in his tent, too. He'd tied her to the tent pole in the centre and chosen to amuse himself with one of the whips the enemy troops used on their horses. He must have been at it for some time, because the short lash had already turned the girl's clothes to ribbons and her exposed skin was a mess of bloody stripes.

"What do you want?" Chao snapped.

To stop this, Yun thought but didn't say. "Numbers for Father. How many dead?"

Chao tucked the whip under his arm and headed for the tiny table in the corner that was already covered in scrolls. He unrolled three before he found the one he wanted, and thrust it at Yun. "Here. Go. If you come back quickly, there might be some girls left for you, too, if we're not through with them yet."

Struggling to keep his expression blank instead of revealing his horror, Yun thanked his brother and hurried out.

For a moment, he stopped beside the pen. The women shrank away from him, as though they'd heard Chao's offer. Perhaps they had.

He glanced around. No one was in view, and his brothers were busy. Yun approached the gate. Any of them could have opened it, for it was latched to keep horses from escaping, not humans. Yet none had.

"Run," he told them, flinging open the gate. "If they catch you, they will kill you."

One woman lifted her head. "We have nowhere to go. They killed everyone else, rounded up us women and…some of us were sent here, while the rest are in the main camp. Entertaining the army." Her accusing eyes told him she knew exactly what that entailed.

"Then die here, or fly and hope to live. The choice is yours, but you are fools if you stay here," Yun said. He turned on his heel and headed deeper into the camp in search of a messenger to carry word home of their victory.

Behind him, a dozen frightened birds flew from their coop. Yun hoped that the ancestors would watch over the escaped girls, even if they weren't his people. They deserved to fly free and not die slaves.

The sounds of revelry drifted through the camp. It seems that the soldiers had discovered the other girls, the ones his brothers had rejected. No doubt all the messengers were taking their turns along with the other men.

Was there something wrong with Yun that he liked his women willing, he wondered. For if the rest of the army derived so much pleasure from striking fear into feminine hearts, surely the fault lay with him.

He did not belong here.

Yun himself would carry word to his father. Leave this stinking battlefield and its sickening pleasures to those who enjoyed such things. Yun would ride for home, and do everything in his power to persuade his father to call off this war.

And as Yun rode off, startling clouds of crows which had already begun to feast on the bloated corpses, he swore that he would rather be among them than become like his brothers.

Three

Bright light beat at Ava's eyelids. She groaned softly. She must have overslept, and now someone had come to fetch her to breakfast.

"Who is she?" a male voice asked.

Ava jerked awake. Men didn't belong in the harem. She sat up, pulling her robes tight around her, and found she was the focus of a dozen pairs of staring eyes.

"Ava," she managed to say, in a voice so small a mouse would be ashamed to own it.

"Look at the cloth. That's silk. She must be

a maid to some great lady, if she gets to wear silk." The speaker thrust his face close to Ava's. "What are you doing here, serving maid? Don't you know a soldiers' camp is dangerous? Or did you meet your sweetheart here last night?"

Loud laughter rang out.

Ava tucked herself up smaller. If she could have magicked herself invisible, she would have.

"Who were you meeting, girl?" an authoritative voice demanded, and the laughter died. A soldier more richly dressed than the others stepped forward. "Tell me his name!"

"I wasn't meeting anyone," she whispered, feeling tears form. She wasn't used to being shouted at.

"Then tell me the name of your mistress. She will get his name out of you, I have no doubt."

Ava shook her head. "I am no one's mistress. I am a maiden, sir." Her cheeks grew hot. A maiden among so many men – this was why she should have stayed in the harem. "My sisters…" She stopped, not willing to draw Lagle and Bianca into her predicament. Perhaps they had made it back to the harem already, missing her in the dark, thinking she had already left.

"What about your sisters?" the man in charge asked.

"They will miss me at breakfast," she admitted. "They will search the harem for me. Perhaps they are already. It is past breakfast, I think."

The man muttered a curse, then pointed at two men. "Batu, Esen. Take her to the harem, and find out who her mistress is. When she is safely inside, return with names."

Both men bowed. "Yes, General."

Batu offered his arm to help Ava to her feet. At first, she hesitated, then realised if she didn't accept his assistance, these men might take hold of her and carry her back. She rested her fingers lightly on his arm and leaped to her feet, breaking the contact before she was burned by it. For she would be, she was certain of it – to touch a man or be touched by him was to be changed forever.

She rubbed her tainted fingertips against her skirt, hoping that such a tiny, brief contact wouldn't be enough to change her. She scarcely had any place in the harem as it was. Where would she go if they threw her out?

The doors to the women's palace loomed like they never had before. Two guards stood sentinel, relaxing in relief when they spotted Ava.

"You found her!" the guard on the left said.

The soldiers exchanged glances. "We did."

"Where?" Right asked eagerly.

Batu said, "By the barracks pool."

The guards bowed low. "Princess, how did you get to the barracks?"

She could not betray her sisters. Ava shook her head. "I do not know. I woke up and there were men…" She shuddered and her voice died.

"Tell the Queen she is found. Summon

servants to help the Princess. Quickly!" Left said to someone inside the palace.

"Princess." The soldiers seemed to realise it at the same moment, sinking to their knees and touching their foreheads to the tiles.

Ava wanted to sink through the floor. "I'm tired. I want to sleep," she lied. Anything to get her out of their sight.

"Come, Princess," said a female voice. Two wide-eyed maids took her arms and led her into the palace.

Ava was too weak to protest as she was taken to her chamber, undressed, and put into bed.

She wasn't changed, she told herself. She wasn't.

But she couldn't help thinking of the soldier she'd touched, however briefly. Batu, that was his name. He'd rubbed his arm as he walked away, with a stunned look of something like awe on his face. She might not be changed, but Batu would not forget this day. She lay back and wished she could forget.

Four

Dirty from long days of travel, Yun knew he could not bathe until he had delivered his report. So he made his weary way to the throne room and prostrated himself at his father's feet.

The petitioner who Yun had interrupted nudged Yun's leg with his foot. "What is the meaning of this? Who is this ruffian?" he demanded.

A country baron who had never been to court before, Yun guessed.

"I am Prince Yun Bataar, your youngest son, Divine Emperor," Yun said. "Please forgive my dishevelled state. I bring news of the battle on our southern borders. Our armies were victorious once more, with numerous enemy slain." He proffered the scroll Chao had given him. "A report from Prince Chao."

"Get up and give it to me," Father said wearily, holding out his hand.

Yun jumped to his feet and ascended the dais to his father's side. "It was a slaughter," Yun said. "I'd be surprised if Chinggis can field a proper army after that, we've killed so many of them. If it were up to me, we'd call off the war here and now. No more fighting."

"And what about their attacks in the south-eastern villages? Baron Dong tells me he has no one left to plant next season's crops, for they are all dead. Chinggis has an army, and they outnumber us. If we stop fighting, their victory is assured, which is why this war will continue as long as I or Chinggis lives. Only a fool would think of stopping." Father eyed

Yun darkly. "But you have always been a fool, writing songs and poems when your brothers were learning to rule. Good thing you are the youngest son and you will never be Emperor. If you were to rule in my place, the empire would fall." He laughed, and was echoed a moment later by the rest of the court.

When the empire's army was too busy raping the women of one village to save their own people, perhaps it deserved to fall.

Yun gritted his teeth, biting back the retort he wanted to make. He'd learned everything his brothers had, and he was far from a fool. Which was why he held his tongue.

"You may return to the army and tell your brothers they have done well, but they need to march for the south-east at once."

Where his brothers would find no sign of Chinggis' army, so they would cross the border to slaughter another village in the name of retribution. And procure more women...

Yun tasted bile in the back of his throat. He had no desire to watch his brothers torment people who had done nothing to deserve it. Better to be a court fool than a dishonourable soldier.

But his father wouldn't want to hear a word against his favourite sons.

"Oh, but I couldn't!" Yun exclaimed in feigned horror. "Not after my first campaign. I must compose an epic poem about our most recent victory while it is still clear in my mind!" He wanted to cringe at how foolish he sounded. Surely his father wouldn't believe...

The Emperor clapped his hands. "That's my boy! After their first battle, your brothers all wanted another one, but you want a poem, and you shall have it! Never let it be said that I don't treasure my sons. You write what you will, and you may perform it when your brothers return victorious." He waved at a nearby servant. "Go with the prince, and make sure my boy has everything he needs."

Yun muttered his thanks and bowed briefly before he fled the court, with the servant close behind.

More than ever, he wanted to vomit. How could he create something that glorified torture and slaughter, when he wanted to stop it?

Perhaps he was a fool after all.

Five

Ava expected to be summoned to her father's throne room at any moment, but as the day dragged on, boredom overtook fear in her mind. There was nothing in her sleeping cubicle but the bed, and lying on it didn't bring her any rest. Curse her for falling asleep last night.

What would her punishment be? If it involved incarceration in a chamber as small as this one, she would lose her wits within the week. She could feel them slipping even now...

Someone threw open the door and Ava blinked in the light, trying to focus on the person who stood in the doorway. "You are to come with me," a female voice said, gesturing imperiously.

Ava clambered to her feet and followed the woman she did not know to a part of the women's palace that was forbidden to her, and, in fact, most of the other princesses: the Queen's apartments.

As the King's principal wife, her apartments were as big as the rest of the harem the other women shared, and the two were separated by a set of double doors that looked gold, or gold-skinned, at least. Her father had conquered enough territory to own solid gold doors, if he so chose, Ava knew, but she wasn't sure why he would want them here, where few people would see them. Why, only the Queen, and the Queen's servants ever entered these chambers. If the King wanted any of his wives or concubines, he summoned them to his own chambers.

"She awaits you inside," the serving woman said.

Ava took a deep breath and pushed open those gleaming doors, then stepped through. Rich carpets covered the floors here, all the way up to a dais where the Queen lounged on a pile of cushions. A throne room without a throne, for the Queen's power came not from a chair but a bed.

Ava shivered. The most powerful woman she knew only had power because she opened her legs to a powerful man, so that she might bear his children. Was that the best destiny she could aspire to? If importance came at the price of letting some man paw her, then Ava didn't want to be significant. Men could keep their hands and all their other parts to themselves, as far as she was concerned. At least her body would be her own.

Unless the man were one who was so awed by her, like Batu had been, that his every touch, his every caress, was like a paean of worship to a goddess.

Ava almost laughed aloud at the thought. She was no goddess. She was barely even a princess, for her mother had been only a concubine, and the King could have chosen not to acknowledge her as his daughter. If she was the goddess of anything, it was shyness. A deity so minor, no one ever noticed her to pray to her, which was probably a good thing.

Ava reached the foot of the dais and bowed low, touching her forehead to the floor, then waited.

"So you are the girl who escaped the harem to seduce some common soldier," the Queen said.

It was on the tip of Ava's tongue to tell her the whole expedition had been Lagle's idea, but she kept her mouth firmly shut. The Queen hadn't asked her to speak, let alone rise, yet.

"But what more could one expect? Your mother was little more than a common whore when she seduced my husband on the battlefield. That he brought her here to the harem was an insult to all the noble-born wives who had to share it with her. And you!" The Queen surveyed Ava, her lip curled in disgust. "Running off to the barracks at the first opportunity! You can't be kept in the harem with the other, more virtuous princesses."

"Like Lagle?" Ava retorted before she could think to close her mouth.

The Queen pounced. "Exactly! You should be trying to emulate my daughter. In fact, that is exactly what you will do. Henceforth, you shall be her lady-in-waiting so that you learn how a proper princess behaves."

Like a spoiled brat, Ava thought darkly but mercifully managed not to say. At least she wouldn't be forced to serve Lagle for long. Her sister's upcoming nuptials were common knowledge. The Queen wouldn't want her…

The Queen continued, "You will accompany Lagle to her husband's palace when she marries, for she must have attendants. That should keep you out of trouble, and far from the young princesses who might be corrupted by your bad example. Lagle is too far above you to sully herself in such things."

Ava's mouth dropped open and she couldn't seem to close it. Leave the harem as Lagle's servant? Did the Queen not know her daughter at all?

Evidently not.

"You had best pack your belongings. Lagle leaves within the week."

Coldness settled over Ava. Exile. She had thought the Queen would send her to the Summer Palace, as rumour said she did with any other princess who irritated her. But sending her to a foreign court with Lagle would be much worse.

"Consider yourself lucky, girl. There are dozens of other highborn girls who would be honoured to serve Lagle when she becomes a queen in her own right. If you do not thank me, I will think you terribly ungrateful."

"I thank you, Your Majesty," Ava said dully.

"You may go."

Ava backed out of the Queen's presence with all haste. It was only when the golden doors closed behind her that Ava dared to breathe again. Her shoulders drooped as her heavy fate settled on them.

Exile with Lagle. Horrors.

Perhaps life imprisonment wouldn't have been so bad. Too late now.

Ava sighed, and accepted her fate. What choice did she have?

She hurried back to the harem to find Bianca, her only friend, and tell the other girl what had happened.

Six

Yun stared at the blank piece of parchment, but he didn't see it. Instead, he saw the pale faces of the girls shut in that horse enclosure, blank and awaiting their fate. Or the corpses of their dead men, who died fighting to save them. Died, and failed.

Farmers. Peasants. Not fighters.

Their daughters and wives. Dead now, like their menfolk, he had no doubt.

He rose from his stool and paced the room.

He wished he'd never gone to war. Never

killed, never seen the aftermath. Never seen the monsters his brothers became. But it was too late for wishes now. Wishes could not bring back the dead whose vengeful spirits would haunt him until the day he died, and maybe afterwards in hell, too.

How could he glorify the slaughter he'd seen?

Yun didn't have words to describe it, and the pictures in his head would not let him rest.

He plunged the brush into the ink and yanked it out again, splattering the table with black spots. Dried blood, he thought, as he swiped the brush across the page. Dead faces with eyes that stared, dead eyes in living faces, and still he heard their screams. He drew their essence on the paper in stark black lines until there was no pristine paper to soil with the people of his nightmares.

And still it was not enough.

Yun sank to the floor, cradling his head in his hands.

He was a fool, like his father said. A fool to

have gone to war, a fool to have come home again.

For one heartsick moment, he wished he was more like his brothers. Capable of revelling in the suffering of others, taking pleasure in causing it.

Then sanity returned.

Yun grabbed the sheets littering the table, crumpling them into a ball against his chest. He pitched the papers into the fire, watching the flames flare up and consume his creations. If only the fire could consume his visions as well. He would welcome hell after death if it could make him forget.

Seven

"You're going where?" Bianca exclaimed.

"To the nether hells, where I'll have to serve Queen Lagle," Ava repeated.

Bianca shook her head. "I don't understand. Why? Lagle doesn't even like you. Why would she ask for you to accompany her to her new court?"

"Because of last night," Ava admitted.

Bianca clapped her hands to her mouth. "You mean you were caught coming back? Is that why no one could find you this morning?

Last night, when we finished swimming, Lagle said she saw you leave, so we should hurry back before we were caught."

"I fell asleep in the garden and when I woke up this morning, the courtyard was full of soldiers."

Bianca paled – quite a feat, seeing as her skin was the palest of any of the princesses already. "Surrounded by men? What did you do?"

Not wanting to admit the embarrassing truth, Ava asked, "What would you have done?"

"I would have done my best to disappear," Bianca began, then stopped. "Run, of course. What did you do?"

"I…" Ava reddened. "I tried to disappear, but there were so many of them. I'm no witch, who can make myself invisible at will." From the way Bianca avoided her eyes, Ava suspected her sister knew more of such things than she did. More than once, she'd seen a shimmer of magic around Bianca. "I did what I always do. I fell to pieces. I'm not brave like you, or even Lagle. They marched me back here until the Queen summoned me to tell me my punishment. Hell serving Lagle."

"How many soldiers were there?" Bianca demanded.

"Dozens. I didn't think to count them."

Bianca waved her hand in dismissal. "Any girl surrounded by a dozen men, let alone more than that, would be crazy not to be afraid. Yet you must have done the right thing, for they didn't hurt you, did they? Against a dozen men, I'm sure I wouldn't have your presence of mind. You are as brave as you need to be. As brave as Lagle, or me, or any one of us. You are our father's daughter, and he fears nothing."

Ava managed a watery smile. "Sometimes I wonder."

Bianca shook her head. "Don't. You were born here, which makes you one of us. The daughter of a slave, a concubine, a wife or a queen, it doesn't matter — you are the daughter of the King. A princess in your own right. In any foreign court, that makes you Lagle's equal, and don't let her airs and graces fool you. She is no better than any of us." She grasped Ava's hand. "Once you leave here, forget everything you thought you knew of harem politics. You are a princess, and you bow to no one but your king and your husband. And who knows? Maybe a husband awaits you, too – Lagle might marry the king, but he could have brothers or sons who are worthy of you. They will not notice a servant…but they will notice a princess who stands proud. The Queen might think this a punishment, but she is wrong. This is freedom for you. I only wish I could be so lucky."

Ava's fingers tightened around Bianca's. "Come with me. Please."

Bianca bowed her head. "I cannot. The Queen's attention fell on me today while we searched for you, and she chose to send me away, too. I leave for the Summer Palace."

"No!"

Bianca smiled sadly. "Yes. It is not so bad. Without you here, I should be lonely. At least at the Summer Palace, I will have the company of other banished sisters. Hazel was sent there, I believe. And Brenna. There is a lake there, I have heard, where we may swim in summer."

Swimming. Not something Ava ever wanted to do. "You will like that," she said grudgingly.

"Only if you promise to make the most of this wondrous opportunity, too. Swear to me that you will not be a mouse any more. Once you leave this palace, you will have the courage and strength of a koi, swimming upstream. No matter how high the waterfall, you will leap to the top. Promise me!" Bianca insisted.

Ava choked out a laugh. "You want me to promise to be a fish?"

"The bravest, most determined fish, who will one day become a dragon, while the rest of us must swim in the stream. Sumi would want this for you, though she is among the ancestors now. Be the fish who flies, Ava." The entreaty in Bianca's eyes brought Ava to tears.

"I will," Ava swore. "By our shared ancestors, and my mother, I swear to you that I will do everything in my power to leave the mouse behind. For you, I will be a leaping koi."

She only hoped she would have the strength to keep her promise.

Eight

"What ails you, Little Fish?"

Yun turned in surprise to find his mother standing in the doorway to his apartment. She hadn't called him that name for a very long time.

He dropped his brush on the table. "It seems I cannot write poetry any more."

The Empress waved her hand airily. "Who can? It is a fine thing for a boy to play with, but you are a man now. A man who has been to war, and come back alive. Not many can say that." She eyed the drawings scattered across the table.

Yun rushed to cover the corpses, but it was too late. His mother had seen all. "Forgive me, Mother. These are not something an empress should see."

"It's not something anyone should see," she said. "What you need is a distraction."

Yun wasn't sure whether he wanted to laugh or cry. What in the world had he not yet tried that could possibly take the battlefield out of his brain?

"A wife would keep you busy."

Yun stared. "A what?"

The Empress's eyes were calculating. "A wife. There are plenty of unwed girls in the palace, daughters to members of the court. Your father gets a dozen petitions every week to let you wed one of them. He thinks you are a boy still."

"No one who has survived a battle like that one is a child. The things I have seen…" Yun shuddered. "Mother, I am a man, but a broken one. What use would I be to a wife? How could I look at her without seeing..." He swallowed. He couldn't tell her about the girls his brothers raped. There were some things no empress should know.

"You are not your brothers," Mother said sharply. "If you treat your wife as they have done theirs, you will no longer be welcome to visit me."

His mother's apartments and pleasure garden were the only place he could find peace, if for a few moments, and she knew it.

"Is there anything you do not know about what goes on in the palace, Mother?" Yun asked.

Mother sniffed. "I am the Empress. There had better not be, or my spies are remiss in their duties. What do you want in a wife? Young? Or closer to your age? Court raised, or from one of the provinces? Pretty, of course, to please your artist's eye. What of her disposition? You are not likely to frighten a girl into obedience, like your brothers, so I suppose you will want one who is already quite docile. Perhaps one with skill in healing, who can help you sleep. Or would you prefer her to be able to sing you to sleep?"

Dizzied by details, Yun shook his head. "Mother, you ask too much. If I must have a wife, my only measure of feminine perfection is yourself, and there can only be one Empress."

Mother narrowed her eyes. "Don't be foolish. A girl fit to be the next empress after me would never be content to marry a youngest son. She would push you to be more ambitious, to make your father name you heir instead of your brothers. She would twist you into a man who is not my son."

"Ancestors forbid any woman try to take me away from you, Mother," Yun said. "So it is best if I do not take a wife at all. What would I need one for, anyway? Father would only send my sons to war and my daughters to marry men he wishes to honour. My brothers can sire such children on their wives. No need for me to get involved."

"No, I should find a girl for you. You will choose wrong. My spies tell me things you will never know until it is too late," Mother declared. "It is settled, then. I will find you a wife, and you will marry her."

Yun sighed. There was no point arguing with the Empress. "Yes, Mother."

Nine

On the morning of her departure, Ava was surprised to find both Bianca and Bianca's mother, Militsa, in the courtyard, among the milling horses and men.

"What are you doing here?" Ava asked.

Militsa smiled indulgently. "On the day both my daughters leave the shelter of the palace for the wide world, I wouldn't be anywhere else."

Ava ducked her head. She wasn't Militsa's daughter, not truly, and no one could mistake them for kin. Militsa's ice-pale hair, only a shade lighter than Bianca's, marked her for what she was: a daughter of a chief from one of the tribes in the far north, taken as a hostage to ensure her father's good behaviour. With a courage Ava found hard to emulate, Militsa had turned her captivity to her advantage, becoming one of the King's concubines. She had been friends with Ava's own mother, Sumi, during the brief time Sumi lived in the harem, and when Sumi lay in a welter of blood on her birthing bed, she had placed Ava in Militsa's arms and begged her friend to take care of the baby. If it weren't for Militsa's kindness, Ava might have died alongside her mother.

"I'm going, too," Bianca said cheerfully, interrupting Ava's reverie. "Our father's guards will escort us to the border, which you and Lagle will cross alone, for the city is not far, and while the Emperor's troops might attack a party of fighting men, they would not harm two highborn women, travelling alone. The guards will take me to the Summer Palace, for there are tales of discharged soldiers and other disreputable men who prey on travellers who take the army roads, as we must. No common soldier shall have me!" She waved her hand and it seemed to Ava that a silvery glow enveloped her fingers.

A glow Ava had seen before, though others had not. Sometimes, when Bianca sneaked through the harem unseen, such a glow had encompassed her whole body. Magic, somehow enhancing her ability to hide. Bianca had never spoken of it, and Ava had never been brave enough to ask, but Bianca's mother's eyes missed nothing.

Militsa embraced Ava, in the fashion of the northern tribes, for such things were foreign to Ava's own people. Yet she endured it, because she knew it was Militsa's way of showing her love. "Watch for evil magic," Militsa whispered. "The Queen's daughter has no magic of her own, but the Queen will not send her to a foreign court without a spell or two to protect her, and possibly more besides. For all this talk of a marriage alliance bringing peace, I fear this one will only escalate the war."

Ava opened her mouth to ask what Militsa meant, but the woman pulled away and nodded toward Lagle and her mother, who had finally deigned to join the travelling party.

The guardsmen bowed as the two ladies passed, before returning to the business of readying the horses for the ride. So it was only the three women who noticed the exchange between the Queen and her daughter.

Lagle struggled into the saddle, even with the aid of a mounting block. She was no horsewoman, thought Ava as she stroked her own mount's flank. The women's palace had included a small stable and a park in which they might ride. Granted, the park was too small for the ponies to move faster than a sedate walk, but Lagle had not set foot in there for as long as Ava could remember. As she and Bianca rode every day the weather was fine, Ava guessed this meant Lagle had not sat astride a horse before. Falada, a great grey horse that contrasted strongly with the others' much darker mounts, shifted from foot to foot under Lagle's weight, as though trying to decide whether she could be bucked off.

A groom caught the beast's bridle, forcing it to stand still.

"A gift for you, which you must wear always," the Queen said, handing something up to Lagle. It appeared to be a necklace, for the girl slipped it over her head and the pendant sat on her breast, glowing red. "As long as you wear it, you will never forget who you are, where you came from, and what you must do." At her words, it flared brighter.

"I will never forget," Lagle said, tossing her head. The horse copied her, nearly unseating her, if it weren't for the groom's grip on the animal. When Lagle regained her balance, she tugged her cloak forward, hiding the necklace from sight.

Ava turned to ask Militsa and Bianca whether they'd seen the strange glow, but they had moved across the courtyard to stand beside Bianca's horse. As she watched, the mother and daughter embraced before Bianca leaped lightly into her saddle. Her horse danced beneath her, but Bianca merely patted the mare's neck and it settled.

Ava's turn. She leaned into her horse's flank, breathing in the animal's warm scent to reassure her. She wasn't afraid, she told herself. She wasn't. Ava swung into the saddle, taking courage from the mare's steady strength. She would be brave, just like she'd promised.

Bianca brought her mount beside her. "Thinking fishy thoughts, sister?" she asked.

Brave, fishy thoughts. "Indeed," Ava said.

"Form up!" the guard captain bellowed. "We're heading out!"

Ava obediently nudged her horse to walk in step with Bianca's as the troop moved out.

"Time for a new adventure," Bianca said, grinning. She always did like listening to tales, though some of them terrified Ava. Heroes and battles and monsters and...

Ava shuddered.

"Fishy thoughts," Bianca reminded her.

"Fishy thoughts," Ava echoed. She managed a wan smile. "Bring on the adventure."

Ten

"You should choose her, Little Fish," Gang said, nodding at a girl who didn't look more than six years old. He chortled. "She's probably all you can handle."

"No, that one!" Chao said, pointing at the child's nursemaid, who looked older than Mother. "Much more obedient. Our Little Fish needs a docile bride, for he is not used to command."

Yun glowered at his older brothers before a quelling look from the Emperor silenced them for a moment as they lined up on either side of him.

Then Gang said, "Hurry up and choose one, Little Fish. Mine is barren, and I want to pick her replacement. I will never hear the end of it from Mother if I steal the toy my baby brother wants, so make your choice!"

Oh, as if the pressure from his mother wasn't bad enough. Now he had to worry about what his brothers might do to the girls he hadn't chosen. They could take them as concubines, or discard their wives to take new ones. Whereas Yun could only save one from their clutches. Letting his mother select the girl seemed like a coward's way out.

Their father held court, shooting them occasional glances to quiet them, but his brothers teased him mercilessly. By the end of the day, Yun was thoroughly sick of the very thought of marriage. His brothers had given their verdict on every woman in court and Yun had begun to wonder if there might be a monastery he could retreat to. One where he did not have to marry anyone. He'd be a useless husband, anyway.

Perhaps if he waited long enough, his mother would arrive at that conclusion on her own, and not make him marry anyone.

The thought cheered Yun considerably.

"What are you smiling about, Little Fish?" Chao hissed. "Did you decide on the one with the big boobs? I think I've had her already. No virgin bride, that girl."

Yun prayed that his brother was lying. Deflowering the daughters of their father's courtiers without even taking them as concubines was the height of dishonour.

He almost wished himself back on the battlefield, where he wouldn't have to endure his brothers' taunting.

Almost, but not quite, Yun reminded himself. He was sleeping better now, for the visions of war were fading a little, but he was still no closer to the epic poem he'd promised his father.

No wife, no poem…was his life destined to

hold anything important? Yun doubted it. After all, the eighth son of the Emperor was so far from the throne, he was nobody, really. A nobody in nice clothes. Fate had been so generous to his brothers, she'd had little left for him. Perhaps he should just be grateful for the crumbs he had. Paper to write his poetry on. Perhaps one day he would write something worth keeping.

Eleven

Ava's horse settled into a fluid canter that at first had her hanging on for dear life, before she realised that the mare knew what she was doing and had no intention of losing her rider. Only then did Ava relax and enjoy it, as Bianca seemed to do, judging by her wide smiles.

For the first time in her life, Ava felt free. Free of fear and free of the harem that had imprisoned her so completely without her even realising it. If only she could ride like this forever, like her chestnut mare wanted to.

All too soon, the captain called a halt. Ava couldn't see past all the mounted men in front of her, so it came as a surprise when Bianca grabbed her round the middle in a hug.

"Stay safe, and be brave. Today you fly free. Fishy thoughts, Ava," Bianca murmured before she released her.

A lump formed in Ava's throat. "You, too," she whispered.

Would she ever see Bianca again?

"This way, Princess," the captain said, beckoning for Ava to follow him.

Yes, she was a princess. Lagle's equal, now she had left the harem. Ava straightened her spine and held her head high.

The path the captain indicated might once have been a road as wide as the one they now travelled, but it was now so overgrown it seemed little more than a track, and a narrow one at that. Ava started forward.

"I must go first," Lagle said haughtily, shoving past Ava.

Ava's mare moved out of Falada's way,

allowing the larger animal to pass. The captain lined up four packhorses behind Ava, all roped together, before he fastened their lead rope to Ava's saddle. At the captain's nod, Ava nudged her mount along the path Lagle had taken, and she heard the captain order the packhorses to follow.

She hoped Lagle knew the way, and that it would not be too long, for the wooded path was surprisingly dark and cool on what had seemed such a hot day. Ava longed for a drink, but she did not know where to find one. Perhaps there would be a stream, or the city would be close. In the harem, it would have been a simple matter of summoning a servant, but there would be no servants until they reached their destination, so Ava plodded on in Lagle's wake.

Finally, Lagle came to a stop at the edge of a river. The current ran fast, but it appeared to be shallow enough at this point to be forded, what with the track ending here and starting up again on the far bank.

Ava looked longingly at the water, and her horse seemed to share her thoughts, for the mare ambled up to the riverbank and stuck her nose in the river.

Thinking the other horses would need a drink, too, Ava slid to the ground and untied them. They lined up alongside hers, slaking their thirst, and she envied them. But not for long.

Ava rummaged through her saddlebags and found the silver cup Militsa had given her for a parting gift. She found a spot upstream of the horses, and dipped her cup. The water was so cold she cried out as it froze her fingers, but that didn't stop her from lifting the brimming cup to her lips and drinking deep. Then refilling it for another drink.

"Fetch me some water," Lagle ordered.

Ava considered offering the full cup to her sister, but another sister's words came to mind, that she and Lagle were equals now, so she drank instead. And a third time. Only then did she fill the cup for Lagle. As she held up the glittering goblet, Lagle's blow struck it out of her hand, spilling the contents at her feet.

"Not in your plain cup, you fool! In my golden one," Lagle insisted.

Ava stooped to pick up her precious cup, pausing to check that its fall hadn't dented the soft metal, before she answered, "And where is your cup?"

Lagle waved languorously at the pack horses. "With my things."

"Then you can get it, and fetch your own water," Ava said slowly. Oh, it almost hurt to force such words out. But she'd promised Bianca to be brave, and here she was. "If you don't want mine, I shall go back to quenching my own thirst."

Deliberately, Ava returned to the riverbank and refilled her cup once more, though she didn't really want another drink. She sipped slowly, all the same, knowing it would goad Lagle into action.

Lagle let out a furious shriek, followed by a string of insults that grew louder with each word she uttered. Ava had never heard such foul language, and neither had the packhorses, it seemed, which bolted in fright.

"Get me a DRINK!" Lagle screamed over the thunder of hooves, stabbing a finger in the direction that the horses had fled. Like a tantruming child, she flailed her arms and drummed her heels against the sides of her horse. Falada leaped into action, like any well-trained warhorse, and charged across the river. Lagle shrieked again and yanked hard on the reins, bringing Falada up short. Lagle kept going, though, right over the horse's head and face-first into the river.

For a moment, Ava froze, not sure whether to laugh or ask Lagle if she was all right. When the girl didn't surface, Ava had her answer, and she waded into the river, careless of the water seeping into her boots. She might not like Lagle, but she wasn't about to let the girl drown.

Ava dragged Lagle to shore, where her sister coughed up a great deal of water, but she didn't wake. A trickle of blood ran down Lagle's face from under her hair, so she must have hit her head when she fell, Ava decided. The pendant around her neck had smashed in the fall, too, leaving little more than a few shards of broken glass tangled in the ribbon. A drop of what looked like blood remained on the stopper, glowing red like the whole thing had before. Ava knew little about magic, but one thing she knew for sure: magic was fuelled by blood, and a single drop was enough to cast a powerful spell. If the bottle had been full of a witch's blood, the spell it cast could have untold consequences.

Or it could simply have been a protection spell to keep her daughter safe. Everyone knew that the Queen doted on her daughter as much as she spoiled her.

But if the spell was evil instead…it could risk the very peace she and Lagle were supposed to secure for their people.

Ava closed her eyes and made a decision. Pulling the necklace over Lagle's head, she pitched it into the river.

She tried shaking her sister awake, but Lagle just lay there, lifeless. Or as lifeless as she could be when she still drew breath.

Finally, Ava persuaded Falada to lie down beside his rider, so that Ava could shove her unconscious sister onto the animal's back. Using the rope the packhorses had left behind, she tied her sister into the saddle as best she could so the girl wouldn't fall off, and tethered Falada's reins to her own mount.

Facing the river, Ava took a deep breath. Fishy thoughts, she told herself. It was her turn to lead.

So Ava led the way into the water.

Twelve

Between his brothers and the words that just wouldn't come, Yun needed an escape. So in a fit of frustration, he begged his father to allow him to do guard duty with the rest of the palace garrison. Marching up and down the walls would make him feel more martial, he'd said, or some such nonsense. Yet, to his surprise, his father had agreed.

Which was why Yun was the first man to spot the strange packhorses.

They came galloping up to the walls as

though all the demons in hell pursued them, lathered like they'd been running for some time. Eyes rolling in panic, they'd been too tired to do more than stand by the bridge, their sides heaving beneath their panniers. When no one appeared to take charge of them after several minutes, Yun headed down to investigate.

It took him some time to calm the beasts enough to take the bridle of the nearest, but as his fingers closed on the leather he froze. The bridle he held wasn't the sort of craftsmanship he normally saw in the empire. The intricate braiding proclaimed it the work of the Horse People. He'd seen enough of it at war. So what were some of their pack beasts doing here now?

Yun unfastened the nearest bag. It was full of silks – women's clothes, and finery, at that. He checked them all, but he found nothing more aside from some jewels stowed beneath the silk, and other such trinkets. But where were the women who owned them? Fine ladies didn't travel without an armed escort. Especially in times of war.

He left the horses in the care of some stablehands, and carried the bags up to his mother's chambers, where he left them to go and search for her. He didn't need to look for long – she was feeding the birds in her private garden.

The brilliant coloured songbirds descended into anarchy like a flock of common sparrows when they spotted a particularly tasty morsel. Mother chided them, but her voice was drowned out by the chorus of squawks as they fought for a piece of fruit.

"Mother, I must ask your advice on a strange matter," Yun began, not sure how to continue.

"Is it about a strange girl?" Mother's smile made him wonder if she could read his mind.

Yun bowed his head. "I fear if there is a girl, something terrible has befallen her. I found her belongings on the backs of horses that came from the Horse People. Highborn, certainly, but nowhere to be found. Mother, has anyone fled the city of late that you know of?"

Mother's eyes narrowed. "One of your brothers' wives, perhaps? I know of no other who would want to. But I know of none who have been missed, either. Let me see the girl's things."

Yun led her to the pile of bags, and Mother summoned a servant to unpack their contents. Gown after gown was held up for the Empress's inspection, but she only shook her head.

"I have never seen a girl wear such gowns, in court or elsewhere," Mother said. "She is not one of your brothers' brides, or one of the girls at court. Perhaps someone's wife as they fled the borderlands for the safety of the city, but were attacked on the way."

"But if they were attacked by Horse People, they could not have been but a few miles from the city. How could they come so far within our borders without us knowing?" Yun asked.

"And if the horses belong to Horse People, where are the people now?"

Mother bit her lip. "Your father is a fool to dismiss you, for you have more wits than he will ever know. Yet I cannot answer your questions, any more than you can. Leave these things with me, for if their owner arrives, I will no doubt hear of it before you do. Return to the wall, and be vigilant. If there truly are Horse People so close to the city, we cannot be too careful."

Yun rose. "I should tell the Emperor."

Mother shook her head. "Tell him what? You have found some horses and gowns with no owner? He will dismiss them as easily as he dismisses you. Find one of the Horse People and then you will have something to show him. Until then, I fear we are as blind as birds flying in a snow storm. And I do fear for us all."

Yun bowed reverently. "Thank you, Mother. I will do as you say."

"Have you given any more thought to

finding a bride?" she asked wryly.

He bowed lower still. "No, Mother."

"When we have solved the mystery of the missing lady, I will find you a bride."

"As my Empress wishes." Yun touched his forehead to the floor at her feet before rising to go. "In the meantime, I must return to my post on the walls."

Thirteen

Onward Ava plodded, pausing every dozen steps to push Lagle higher onto her horse's back so she would not slip off. She would have given everything she owned to be riding full tilt along the dusty army road with Bianca to the Summer Palace.

The thirst she thought she'd quenched raged again, but she could do nothing about it except hope that the journey would be over soon.

The forest ended as abruptly as it had begun – on the banks of another river, or so it seemed, for this one was wider and deeper than the one they had forded several hours back. There would be no fording this river, so it was a mercy that a wooden bridge spanned the watery barrier that would otherwise keep them from the city.

Until they emerged fully from the forest, trees had hidden the city walls, which rose up higher than those of Ava's father's palace. Why, she could see men marching atop them, armed with bows and spears. Whispering a prayer to the ancestors that the men would not see two women as invaders to shoot at, Ava led the horses onto the old bridge. The paint had long since faded and cracked. Much like the road that led to it, the bridge had fallen into disuse. Perhaps Ava should have prayed for the bridge to hold them so that they might reach the city – never mind the men on the walls.

Falada turned skittish, having to be coaxed over the bridge with soothing words and repeated tugs on the reins before the warhorse would follow Ava to the open city gates. She was so preoccupied with the horses that Ava didn't see the approaching guard.

"HALT!"

The authoritative shout undid all Ava's efforts to calm Falada. The horse reared, throwing Lagle to the cobbles.

The guard who'd presumably shouted jumped clumsily out of the way of the horse's flailing hooves – no mean feat, given he was covered head to toe in armour.

"Get your animal under control!" he growled.

Ava wanted to say that she'd had them under control until he startled them. What kind of barbarians were these people, causing trouble and then blaming her for it? Surely it was a man's job to protect women, not frighten their horses and shout at them.

Unless he was a true barbarian, the kind that would ignore the fact that Lagle lay on the ground, more injured than before.

Ava slid to the ground, keeping a firm grip

on the reins of both horses as her lifeline to the civilisation of home, as she went to where Lagle lay in a crumpled heap. Her head wound had resumed bleeding.

"Look what you've done!" Ava cried, lifting her bloodied hand so he could see it. Tears trickled down Ava's cheeks and she was helpless to stem the flow. Would he throw her to the cobbles next?

"This is a city gate, and it's my job to guard it, mistress, letting no enemies inside," the man said. "Be you friend or enemy?"

"We have done nothing to you. Nothing. And you…she…do you have someone who can help her? If you fetch a physician, someone who knows how to care for her…" Ava dissolved into tears again. She might not like Lagle, but she had no desire to see her sister die.

"Mistress, I am a guard. I can't leave the gate unguarded. My captain would – "

"Berate you if he knew you'd let a woman die while you argued with a girl at the gate," another voice finished for him. The second man wore similar armour to the first, though his seemed to fit him better, with a shine to the leather that caught the sun. "Fetch a physician. I will find out what kind of threat a two-woman army presents to the city." None whatsoever, the dark eye slits of his helm seemed to say.

"Begging your pardon, sir, but if one of the women was Da Ying, she could take the city single-handedly, or so the stories say." The first man hesitated, then bowed. "I will get that physician." He hurried away.

The new man cocked his head as he surveyed Ava. "You're smaller and younger than I'd expect of the legendary Da Ying. But I am told appearances can be deceiving. Is that who you are?"

Ava peered up at the man through the veil of her tears. "I've never heard of her. I am Princess Ava, the daughter of King Chinggis, and we've been sent to forge an alliance with your king." She struggled to lift Lagle off the ground, but she wasn't strong enough. "If she dies, my father is likely to consider this as an act of war if you don't help her!" Her words ended in a sob.

"I think we have more than enough war for two kingdoms right now. Though you might want to remember we have an emperor, not a king, when you meet him." The man crouched beside her, slid his hands under Lagle and lifted her effortlessly into his arms as he straightened. Covered in mud and blood, her clothes torn from two falls, Lagle looked more like a beggar than a princess against the leaping fish tooled across the front of his breastplate. "I will see that your maidservant is cared for. Is there anything else you desire, Princess? Or do you wish to be presented to the Emperor immediately?"

Ava's mouth dropped open. Why would she be presented to the Emperor when Lagle was…was…

She swallowed. Lagle was unconscious, injured, and in no fit state to be presented as an emperor's bride.

"I would like to freshen up, and make myself presentable," she managed to say. If she took long enough, perhaps Lagle would wake and recover sufficiently for an audience with the Emperor.

He nodded. "I'll have some of my men form an honour guard to escort you to the palace, where apartments will be prepared for you." He gestured toward another guardsman, issued his orders, and marched off with Lagle still in his arms.

Ava opened her mouth to protest, but a crowd of men surrounded her, taking the reins from her nerveless fingers. The memory of waking up beside the pool silenced any urge she had to speak. Meekly, she went with them without saying a word.

Fourteen

Yun's favourite part of guard duty was walking the walls, even before his mother had ordered him to do so. Officially, he was watching for invaders, and from that high vantage point he could see so far, some days he could see clear to the mountains, on the rare occasions when they weren't shrouded in cloud. Striding along the walls gave him a sense of purpose, for if war came here, he would happily fight to protect his home.

Today, the mountains hid their crowns, and

the people of the city went about their normal business. All except one woman, by the sound of things, whose shrill voice rang through the streets like a warning bell. Curiosity drove Yun to investigate.

The woman – scarcely more than a girl, judging by her diminutive size – struggled to keep two horses under control while she tried to lift a woman from the ground. A guardsman stood by, speaking to her but not offering her any assistance. Yun hurried down to the gate, shaking his head in an attempt to banish the image that suddenly plagued his mind – one of the women penned up in his brothers' camp. These two were nothing like them, judging by the richness of their clothing under the dust.

Why would two women travel alone? They had not even a single guard to see to their safety. Perhaps they, like Baron Dong, were the sole survivors of an enemy incursion.

The same incursion that had killed the owner of the silk gowns? Yun's blood ran cold. These women still had their saddlebags, so they could not be one and the same.

As Yun approached, it quickly became apparent that the larger girl was unconscious and injured. Sending the guardsman for a physician also gave him the excuse of questioning the girl to assuage his curiosity.

He knelt to lift up the injured girl as he asked the younger one what her name was. If he knew where she was from, Father might be able to send troops there to prevent further bloodshed.

He almost dropped her companion when he heard the girl's name.

"I am Princess Ava, the daughter of King Chinggis." She stood tall and proud, as Yun would expect of his enemy's daughter, and she surprised him again by insisting she came in peace.

Yun was lost for words. He managed to babble something about how he would take care of the unconscious girl, before he remembered himself and asked the princess if there was anything she wished of him. He prayed silently that she would not ask for anything that he, as the Emperor's youngest son, could not deliver.

He breathed a sigh of relief when all she asked for was a place to wash, and an audience with the Emperor.

Yun rounded up a squad of guardsmen to act as her honour guard, sending a runner ahead to make sure an apartment would be prepared for her. He carried the unconscious girl to the palace gates, before passing her to some servants. They could find suitable accommodation for her and see that a physician tended to her injuries, whatever they might be.

He had one last task to complete to keep his promises to the foreign princess. He strode into his father's throne room, whistling a folk song about geese.

The crowd of petitioners parted for him, some more willingly than others. Yun didn't stop whistling until he'd reached the foot of his father's dais, where he sketched a quick bow that he knew would scandalise the courtiers even more.

"Chinggis sent you a gift, Father," Yun said.

The Emperor's tolerant smile turned into an expression of thunderous anger. "More heads? Or hands? If he thinks to butcher my people, he will pay dearly for it."

"Two heads, four hands, attached to two lovely young women, actually," Yun said. "One of them claims to be his daughter."

"And the other?" Father demanded.

Yun shrugged. "Unconscious, and not saying much. I think she might be the Princess's maid."

This only seemed to darken Father's mood. "Keep them apart. Send their belonging to the Empress, and make sure she knows to search them. The Horse People are treacherous by nature and the women are worse than the men. Especially the witches. Did she cast a spell on you? Or touch you at all?"

Yun burst out laughing. "If she'd cast a spell on me, how would I know? And of course I touched the maid. I carried her into the palace, for the unconscious girl couldn't walk, and the Princess was too small to carry her." He sobered when he remembered the Princess. "The Princess seeks an audience with you. I had her shown to a guest chamber so that she might bathe before she comes before you. What am I to say to her when she asks for her clothes? You cannot think to invite her to come to court naked."

Several men laughed, but the Emperor did not.

"Have your mother send something suitable," Father said, waving his hand in dismissal.

Yun considered sending a servant, but his father's attitude toward the Princess and the Empress nettled him. An empress was not some common maid, to paw through a guest's clothing or source a gown for a girl. And the Princess was no witch, he was certain of it. If she was, she would have enchanted the guard and sneaked into the town unseen instead of causing the scene where he'd been forced to intervene.

Yun executed a mocking bow. "As the Divine Emperor wishes, for his smallest whim must be obeyed."

He heard his father's snort as he marched out of the throne room, toward his mother's apartments.

The Empress was waiting, as though her spies had already told her the news. Yun didn't doubt that they had – his mother knew everything that went on in the palace.

"I thought you would be too busy to visit me," Mother said before Yun could even offer a greeting. "Carrying a girl through the city streets into the palace, getting bespelled by witches, and upsetting your father." Mother set down her embroidery. "Are you in love with the girl?"

It was Yun's turn to snort. "The Princess's maid? No."

Mother's eyebrows rose. "So you believe that the girl is a princess, the daughter of

Chinggis?"

Yun considered for a moment. "She didn't bow or lower her eyes or any of the things I'd expect from a lower born woman. And the way she said it...I believed her. If she'd wanted to lie, she would have said she was the daughter of one of our allies, not the daughter of such an enemy. Why, my brothers would have killed her on the spot once they heard her father's name."

"Does this princess know who you are?"

"Everyone knows my armour. Who else carries the leaping fish?"

Mother shook her head. "Everyone in the palace, maybe, but not all of the common people know it. How would a foreign princess know that you are a poor fisherman?"

"I'm not a poor fisherman," Yun protested. "I fished that koi out of the ponds myself, with no help from my brothers. I lay there for hours, waiting for it to take the bait. It was only when I tried to pull it from the hook that it leaped, flying so high it reached the top of the waterfall. It must have swum upstream to the river, for I never saw its like in the palace gardens again."

"None of your brothers would have borne the insult, armour made to immortalise your defeat. Yet you…"

"It's good armour," Yun said. "Chao intended to shame me, I am sure, but the joke was on him when I wore the breastplate anyway. What use is a youngest son but to make his elders laugh? Perhaps I should sharpen my singing skills so that I might entertain you all at dinner." He didn't mean to sound so bitter, but that's the way the words came out.

Mother laid a hand on his arm. Such small fingers were surprisingly heavy when they carried the weight of a mother's love. "You are not useless, Yun. Perhaps you have yet to find your purpose, but I pray it shall reveal itself in time. How goes your poetry?"

"It goes poorly. All I can see is carnage, Mother. The blood on the battlefield. The honour and glory and all the things that go with victory elude me." Despair welled up. He would never be a poet.

"Describe the Princess for me."

Yun hadn't heard right. "What?"

Mother repeated patiently, "Describe the Princess for me. What manner of beast does she remind you of?"

A beast? She was a girl, a woman, not some coarse creature. And yet the idea took root, spreading through his thoughts. "A bird of a girl, small and light and delicate, but with a sharp tongue and a shrill voice." Yun smiled at the memory.

"What kind of bird?" Mother demanded.

"Not an eagle. She is no hunting bird of prey. Yet she is no seed-eating sparrow, either. She is a caged songbird, I think. Her colours do not blaze the brightest, and her song is not the sweetest, but she belongs. Yet from looking into her bright eye, you know she is watching the door, waiting for something to change so that she might be free."

Was she? The vision of the Princess as a bird flying from her cage felt so right, it was hard to doubt it. Yet he did not doubt the vision had leaped fully-formed from his own imagination.

Mother's eyes were upon him, searching his soul, it seemed. "When your father meets this girl, I shall be in court. And so will you."

Yun knew better than to protest. Besides, he'd get to see the Princess again, and see how she compared to the songbird in his imagination.

Fifteen

Ava was led to a sumptuous apartment that would have satisfied the Queen – much too grand for her, Ava wanted to say, but perhaps this kingdom was richer than her father's. This might be an ordinary chamber in an emperor's palace. Lagle was surely just as well accommodated. If not, Ava would soon hear of it, the moment Lagle awoke. For she would wake. She must.

"Do you wish to wash, mistress?" a female voice asked.

Ava whirled, to find a half dozen maids bowing low, each bearing a bundle of fabric. They bowed again in unison.

"Ah…yes," Ava said, looking for a jug and a bowl.

"Follow me to the bath house, mistress," the same voice said, and one of the maids turned and led the way out of the chamber.

When Ava entered the bath house, she wished she hadn't. The ornate bath inside was big enough to swim across, or to hold at least a dozen people. Lagle would love it, Ava was certain. As for Ava herself, she felt the maid's eyes upon her as she forced herself to undress and enter the bath as if she was used to this kind of luxury. To her relief, the water was warmer than the pool outside her father's barracks, so she managed to slip beneath the surface without showing too much of the un-princess-like panic welling up inside her.

At least fishy thoughts seemed more natural in water, she thought to herself as she scrubbed away the dust from the journey.

All too soon, she was clean, and she surrendered her body to the army of maids who had returned. They dried, patted, perfumed and dressed her in finery that she definitely didn't recognise. Judging from the way the maids fluttered around her, up to and including three of them dropping to the floor with needles and thread to raise the hem of her gown, Ava assumed the clothes were new garments made especially for Lagle, who was almost a head taller than Ava and somewhat stouter, too.

Ava considered telling them that they would have to unpick their work when Lagle awoke and demanded her dress back, but she decided against it. Let Lagle give them the bad news. Ava had enough to worry about, being presented to the Emperor and all. Being presented as his possible bride, if Lagle didn't recover.

A shiver ran through her at the thought, one that wasn't entirely unpleasant. What if she was like the heroine in one of Bianca's stories, and the king fell in love with her, naming Ava as his bride instead of Lagle? For one thrilling moment, Ava imagined herself as a queen, no, an empress, seated upon a throne with a crown on her head. Were crowns heavy? With so much gold and jewels, surely it would be a heavy burden on one's head. She had heard that her father preferred a military helmet because it did not weigh so heavily on him as a crown.

If even her father complained of it, then wearing a crown must be a heavy burden indeed. Far too heavy for Ava, a princess so insignificant she would live out her days in service to Lagle.

The weight of this thought brought Ava rapidly out of her reverie. She shook her head, resolving to think braver thoughts, as Bianca had advised her. Lagle might marry the king, but there were surely princes and noblemen who might marry her and whisk her away from her miserable fate as Lagle's maid.

"Does the gown not please you, mistress?"

one of the maids asked, frowning deeply. She gestured imperiously and two maids stepped forward, carrying a mirror between them that was almost as big as Ava herself. "This is the fashion worn by all the great ladies at the Emperor's court, but if you wish to change, we are here to serve, mistress."

Ava scarcely recognised her own reflection. Even in the muted lighting in the bath house, the gold embroidery on her gown glittered, drawing her eye away from the layers of shining silk beneath it. Her hair had been tamed into an elaborate coiffure atop her head, the curlicues reminiscent of a flower opening its petals to greet the dawn. Beneath it all, the maids had painted her face so that her unnaturally pale cheeks resembled Bianca's, while her carmined lips made her think of rosebuds. Yet it was her own eyes that drew her in. Dark and mysterious, the maids had applied layers of powder and paint until her eyes seemed to draw in the spirit of anyone who dared to meet her gaze. Even as her eyes widened in fright, they only appeared deeper and more dangerous. The eyes of a queen, Ava thought uneasily.

Ava assured the maids that everything about her toilette pleased her, for she now looked every bit a queen.

She received a flurry of bowing for the compliment before the maids hustled her back to her apartment, where two impatient guardsmen waited. Not that she could see their expressions or even their faces under their helmets, of course, but the way they hurried her off in a new direction, muttering about how long ago the Emperor had summoned her and how angry he would be at the wait, certainly confirmed it. Ava had to take two steps to every one these guardsmen took, so small was she, but they never slowed, so by the time they reached the ornate bronze doors to the throne room, Ava was out of breath from running to keep up. She would have crashed into the doors when her guards stopped abruptly, if it wasn't for the doors themselves swinging open before her, almost as if by magic. Ava didn't see the telltale glow of a spell, though, and the mystery was solved by the presence of two more guardsmen, standing behind each door.

She stumbled inside, flustered and wishing herself back in the relative peace of the bath house, even before the crowd turned to stare at her. Men and women both, far more richly dressed than she was, their dark eyes seeming to suck at her spirit as she passed them.

Fish had dark eyes, Ava reminded herself, and so did she. She drew herself up, remembering her promise to Bianca, and waited for her name to be announced.

The herald's sonorous shout made her sound far more important than she felt, even if most of the titles he described were her father's and not her own. He made no mention of her mother, which Ava supposed was better than being described as kin to the Queen.

As the herald's words rang out, the stares that had been directed at her now lowered to the floor, as the entire court bowed to a foreign princess. Feeling herself invisible in a hall full of people gave Ava the courage to move forward, something she wouldn't have thought possible a moment before, with all those eyes upon her.

On a dais at the far end of the hall sat the Emperor on his throne, flanked by other people on lesser chairs. Reminded of her father's throne room, which was much smaller, Ava kept her eyes on the floor so that she wouldn't trip on her stately skirts and embarrass herself. When she reached the foot of the dais, she dropped gracefully to her knees, allowing her skirts to fan out around her, before bowing so low her forehead touched the floor.

Princesses bow only to their king and their husband, no one else. Bianca's warning rang in her head, too late.

Ava struggled to rise, but the damage was done. She had subjugated herself before a foreign king. Her face red with shame, she stayed on her knees to hide her embarrassment.

"So, Chinggis sent a witch to bespell me. He thinks I am a coward, to be frightened by a mere child!" the Emperor roared. "Or maybe she is not really a child. The stories say his witch queen casts spells to make her appear more youthful. Perhaps Chinggis is a defiler of children, who likes his girls so young!"

Laughter erupted around the hall, echoing off the walls. Ava's blood simmered.

"Try to cast your spell, witch! My guards will cut you down before you can spread any evil here!" the Emperor continued.

Ava wet her lips. "I'm no witch."

"You lie! Why else are you here? I agreed to meet no envoy of Chinggis!"

It began to dawn on Ava why she and Lagle had been sent across the border without an escort.

"I am here to make peace through an alliance. A marriage alliance," she said carefully.

The Emperor snorted. "An alliance with who?"

"With you." It was on the tip of her tongue to add, "Your Majesty," as she might when speaking to a king, but she wasn't sure what to call an emperor. Lagle would know. That's why she should be here, not Ava.

An ominous silence stretched between them. Ava dared to raise her head, to find the Emperor staring at her.

"I don't need another wife," he said coldly. "My Empress has given me many sons, who have wives and children of their own. Go back where you came from, girl, and tell your witch mother we want none of her kind here."

"I cannot return without…" Lagle, she wanted to say, but instead she said, "without an alliance and a promise for peace."

"Your kind want nothing but war."

Muttering rumbled around the hall as many of the courtiers agreed with the Emperor.

Ava swallowed. "I don't. I want peace. My father wants peace. That's why he sent his daughter here to marry…marry into your family." She didn't dare say that Lagle was here to marry him. Lagle would never agree to be his wife if she couldn't be queen. "If not you, then perhaps one of your sons…?"

Lagle might settle for the crown prince as a husband. Maybe.

Another snort. "Only the child of Chinggis would dare to demand one of my sons in marriage. None of my sons would take you for a wife, or even a concubine. What man wants a viper in his bed?"

Titters came from the crowd, which quickly silenced as footsteps sounded on the stone floor.

"I might. If I survived the night, it would make a wonderful tale to sing at feasts," a familiar voice drawled.

Ava turned her head in time to see an armoured man leap down from the dais. No one, not even the guards beside her, moved to stop him.

"She looks so lovely down there on her

knees. No wonder you're drawing this audience out, Father. When you're done, I'd like her." The man pulled off his helmet, revealing quite a handsome face. He winked at Ava.

The Emperor's eyebrows bunched together. "Better to send her home to her father than risk war or worse."

More muttering came from the crowd.

"But look at her, Father. As pretty as a poem. Just what I want in a wife."

Wife? No, Lagle was the one who was supposed to get married, not Ava, and surely not to this strange prince who spoke of songs and tales and poetry. Surely the Emperor wouldn't change his mind on the whim of his son.

"Are you a virgin?" the Emperor demanded.

Ava blushed scarlet. "Of…of course."

The Emperor turned to his son. "See if she lies, and if she bears a witch mark."

"When I have her alone in my chambers, I will make a thorough investigation," the prince said gravely.

The Emperor gave a curt nod. "Be it on your head, then." He clapped his hands. "Summon a matchmaker. This marriage will happen now or not at all."

Ava's mouth dropped open. Now? But Lagle...

The Emperor's gaze was fixed on her. "Have you changed your mind, daughter of Chinggis?"

Slowly, Ava shook her head. "If a marriage alliance is the price of peace, then I will play my part in it. I will marry the prince...the prince..."

"Yun Bataar," the prince supplied with a sweeping bow. "The eighth son of our Blessed Emperor. Delighted to meet you, Princess Ava."

Lagle would never agree to marry an eighth son. A king, or the heir to the throne, were all she would agree to. Of course, Lagle would probably not permit Ava to marry a prince before she herself was married.

All the more reason to do this now.

"I will marry Prince Yun Bataar as soon as the ceremony can be arranged," Ava said, trying and failing to still the shaking in her voice.

She was about to discover just how quickly that could be.

Sixteen

When the Princess entered the room, her face froze in terror. Yun wanted to get up and tell her everything would be all right, but as he rose from his chair, his mother's hand landed on his arm.

"Don't," she whispered.

While Yun might disagree with his father, he never disobeyed his mother. Reluctantly, he subsided.

When the Princess reached the foot of the dais, she fell to her knees, as though they would no longer carry her. Again, Yun felt his mother's restraining hand on his arm, and again he resisted going to the girl's assistance.

Yun's blood simmered as his father tormented the girl, calling her names while the court laughed. He charged her with crimes that should rightly be laid at Chinggis' door, not his daughter's, but no one else seemed to care.

And then his father called her a witch.

The girl's head jerked up, just enough for Yun to see her eyes flash with fury. "I'm no witch."

Yun almost laughed. If she was a witch, she would have cast a spell then and there on the Emperor. That she didn't was proof of her honesty.

Then she uttered six words that made Yun sit up and listen: "I am here to make peace."

His mouth grew as dry as the desert, while his heart beat faster. Could this girl persuade his father to accept a peace alliance where he had failed?

Suddenly the girl on her knees no longer

looked so subservient. She looked like a snake ready to strike, but choosing to spare him. Because she wanted peace.

Marriage. Why were they talking about marriage? Yun must have missed something. She wanted to marry one of the Emperor's sons?

His belly twisted within him. If any of his brothers got hold of her, they would make her suffer. The pain of the girls they'd tortured to death in that village would be nothing compared to what they'd do to Chinggis' daughter.

"Save her," Mother hissed. "Ask for her."

Yun stared at the Empress, but she only stared implacably back. She had given him an order. One that he must obey.

"What man wants a viper in his bed?" Father demanded.

This time, Mother didn't stop him when Yun rose. Of course not. "I might," he said with forced nonchalance as he strode to his father's side. "If I survived the night, it would make a wonderful tale to sing at feasts."

The Emperor stared at him, lost for words.

But Yun detected a wavering. If his father gave him the girl, perhaps peace would be possible.

Yun continued in the same vein, talking of poetry and nonsense until his father's patience wore thin. Thin enough to concede to what Yun wanted.

"Be it on your head, then," the Emperor grumbled.

Yun held out his hand for the girl's, and for the first time felt the tremors running through her. She truly was terrified, but she had stood up to his father all the same. More than ever, he wanted to save this princess from the rest of his family.

"I am Yun Bataar, eighth son of our Blessed Emperor," he told her. Her face fell, and he stumbled over his polite words about how pleased he was to meet her.

The proud Princess didn't want an eighth son, and who could blame her? But if she knew what the other seven would do to her...

No. Yun would not let his brothers harm her.

"I will marry Prince Yun Bataar," the Princess said, the proud tilt of her chin announcing that she would accept nothing less.

Yun's mind whirled. Hadn't his father offered her as a concubine, a mistress? When had he agreed to make her his wife?

He directed a silent entreaty to his mother, begging her with his eyes to tell him what to do.

The Empress's eyes blazed. She nodded once, a jerk of her head that left Yun with no other choice.

"The sooner I get her alone in my chambers, the better. Thank you, Father," Yun said.

The girl trembled, and Yun wished he could reassure her, tell her she had nothing to fear from him. Not tonight, not ever. But as the Emperor's joke of a youngest son, he had a role to play. So he smiled, and joked, and generally made light of his marriage, even as they said their vows. It wasn't until they reached the privacy of his chamber that he allowed the façade to slip.

He poured himself a drink and downed it in one gulp, before pouring another. Only then did he have the courage to speak to her. His wife.

He turned and opened his mouth, but what he saw left him speechless.

Seventeen

For all the talk in the women's palace about how grand Lagle's wedding would be, with many changes of clothing, complicated ceremonies and public spectacles that Lagle had boasted about endlessly, Ava's wedding to Yun was surprisingly simple. No clothing changes, and the ceremony was so fast she had trouble following it. Surely all she'd done was serve a few cups of tea and sipped at her own before she was bundled out of the throne room for what she thought would be the first change of clothes. It wasn't until the last maid had left that she realised she was alone in a room with Yun and, to her gut-churning consternation, a bed.

Yun poured himself a drink of something that smelled far stronger than the traitorous tea she'd been too busy drinking to notice her own marriage ceremony until it was over. He offered Ava a cup of the pungent liquid, but she shook her head. If she drank a single mouthful, it would only come right back up again. She'd left the only mother and home she'd ever known, with the prospect of a lifetime of servitude to her least favourite sister, and before she'd had time to mourn her loss, her fate had twisted so inexplicably to give her a husband.

Which made her a wife with wifely duties, Ava reminded herself.

Though she was one of the King's daughters, sex was no secret in the women's palace. She knew very well what was expected of her, though she had never expected to need that knowledge until now. Methodically, she removed her clothing, layer by layer, until she was down to her thin shift. She considered removing that, too, but she'd heard that some men preferred to do their own unveiling, especially the first time.

Ava swallowed, climbed onto the bed, lay down, and spread her legs. Closing her eyes, she prayed to the ancestors that Yun's attentions would be over quickly.

"No drink, and straight to business? Are you sure you are Chinggis' daughter?" Yun asked, laughing.

Ava's eyes snapped open. Not a day passed that Lagle hadn't made some scathing comment about her legitimacy. All Ava knew what that her father would never have kept her if he was in any doubt that she was his child.

If Yun doubted it, why had he agreed to marry her?

"I am Chinggis' daughter," Ava said slowly. "And your wife."

The word sounded so strange.

Yun's laughter died. "Yes, which means I have a duty to perform." He began to disrobe, and Ava closed her eyes again. The more she saw of him, the more he would frighten her.

She felt his weight compress the mattress near her feet. Ava risked opening her eyes.

The man who knelt between her legs was magnificent, and with every bit of him on display, she could look her fill. Perhaps she might enjoy a little of her marriage bed, if she could look upon a man like this while he did whatever he wanted with her. Bianca would have loved to marry such a handsome prince.

Bianca would also be braver about her wedding night than Ava, who began to shiver as she remembered what would happen.

Yun lifted his arm, looking determined, and light glinted off metal. The metal of a dagger blade he held poised, ready to stab into her flesh.

Ava screamed.

Yun grunted, then said, "There."

Ava dared to open her eyes. He'd sliced his

hand, and now he held it between her legs, so close the blood almost dripped on her instead of the sheet beneath her. Wide-eyed, all she could do was stare as he let his hand bleed for a long moment, before wiping it on the sheet. His fingers brushed her thigh and she shivered again, but not entirely out of fear this time.

"Go up to the top of the bed, and cover yourself," Yun advised.

Ava scrambled to obey, too confused to do anything else.

Yun ripped the bloodied sheet off the bed and gave a shout of triumph. He threw open the room door and flapped the sheet at the crowd of courtiers waiting outside. "She fought fiercely to start with, but I tamed her. See?" He pointed at Ava, who curled up into a tiny ball at the head of the bed, as far away from the door as possible, then flapped the sheet again. "I should thank Chinggis for his gift of a sweet virgin bride."

The courtiers tittered and the crowd slowly dispersed until only Yun stood in the doorway, no longer holding the sheet.

"Get some sleep," Yun ordered. He wrapped a robe around himself, then left, closing the door after him.

Ava waited, but he didn't return. After a while, she uncurled and allowed herself to relax. Evidently her husband didn't want to share her bed tonight. She would summon up the courage to ask him why later. For now, she stretched out on the bed and fell asleep.

Eighteen

Yun paced the walls, unable to get the image out of his head. Of her, his wife, the pretty princess stretched out on his bed in a shift so thin he could see every delicious detail of her body through it, which should have aroused him beyond belief, if it wasn't for her expression.

Her squeezed shut eyes, her wobbling lip, her clenched fists on either side of her throat…as though she expected to be punished.

What had she done to deserve punishment?

Nothing, he told himself. She wanted peace, the same as he did. She had consented to the marriage, and shown courage when his father had humiliated her before the court. She had even spread her body out on the bed, a sacrifice to this marriage alliance she wanted...but not with him.

I am not my brothers, Yun raged inwardly, wishing he could shout it at the top of his lungs. Everyone already believed he was mad, but until today, they'd have been wrong.

And he didn't dare tell anyone what he'd done. He was a man, and it was his job to shed blood in the name of war and peace. As a woman, she shouldn't need to. So he'd turned his dagger on himself because he couldn't bear to hurt her...and he refused to let anyone suggest the marriage hadn't been consummated. If their marriage dissolved, there would be nothing to stop his brothers from hurting her. As it was...it was only their love for their youngest brother that kept her safe. He prayed that would not change.

As a cold wind started to blow, Yun warmed himself by imagining what it might be like if Ava was willing. If one night he entered his bedchamber and found her with her legs and her eyes open, wearing a welcoming smile. How he would cradle her delicate, birdlike body as he made love to her, eliciting gasps of pleasure from her, not pain. Not just once, but all night, or until she lay in his arms, spent, with a smile on her lips that not even sleep could wipe away.

Bliss, surely.

But not tonight.

So Yun continued to march along the walls, staring out into the darkness for an enemy he could not see, wishing he was in his bedchamber with the lovely woman who had somehow bewitched him without one whit of magic.

Ava, the wind seemed to whisper, but Yun closed his ears to it.

Nineteen

When Ava woke in the morning, she was still alone in the bed. The same maids from yesterday ushered her to the bath house, but today none of them would meet her eyes. In fact, they seemed hesitant to touch her now.

Finally, she couldn't bear it any longer. "What have I done wrong?" she asked. "Yesterday, you were all happy to help me bathe and dress. Today, you act as though Prince Yun's wife is unclean."

The maids exchanged glances for a long

moment, before one of them stepped forward and spoke up.

"A thousand apologies, mistress, but the Emperor's sons are known for their rough use of women, especially their wives. Most new brides in the palace do not wish to be touched the morning after their wedding night, and many of them have ordered us to look away instead of staring at their hurts. After so many new wives screaming at us not to be touched or stared at, we now do this as a matter of course, in order to better serve you. My deepest apologies if this offends, mistress. If you will tell me where your hurts are greatest, we have salves that may help, if you will permit us to apply them."

Ava's mouth dropped open. So it was true and this was a barbarian kingdom. Men who hurt their women instead of protecting them. Her father had never done such a thing to any of his wives or concubines. Oh, she'd heard that a girl's first time could be a little painful, but no new resident to the women's palace ever appeared to have been beaten.

"I have none," Ava said slowly. "Prince Yun was…" Inexplicably merciful? Not attracted to her in the slightest? Unwilling to consummate the marriage while willing to go to great lengths to hide this? Ava settled for, "He was kind."

"His Royal Highness Prince Yun is different to his brothers," the maid who'd spoken admitted. The other girls tittered and some even blushed.

"I must dress to please him better today," Ava said, not realising she'd spoken aloud until the maids brought her another new gown.

"Very good, mistress."

Lagle would not want to marry the crown prince or any of his brothers if they beat women. Why, her head injury from her fall from her horse might be the least of her hurts if she did.

"Where is Lagle?" Ava asked.

"Who, mistress?"

"Lagle, the girl who arrived with me. She

was thrown from her horse and hurt."

More glances were exchanged. "Do we not serve you well enough, mistress, that you wish for your foreign maid?"

Lagle, a maid? Ava hoped no one had said that to Lagle. "I must see her, and know she is well."

"The Emperor commanded that we must serve you, not your foreign maid, in case you mean the empire ill, but he did not say you could not see her," the maid began. "When you are dressed, I will take you to her."

Ava nodded her thanks and submitted meekly to the maids' ministrations. Perhaps if she looked beautiful enough today, Prince Yun would take Ava as his wife properly tonight.

Twenty

Lagle's chamber was as spare and small as Ava's old one at the women's palace. More so, perhaps, as she had no spare clothing or even any belongings to personalise the space. Ava dreaded what Lagle would say when she discovered she'd slept upon a pallet and not the golden feather bed she'd boasted about so many times in the harem.

"Has she awoken?" Ava asked, though she knew the answer before the words had left her lips. If Lagle had awoken before this, the whole palace would have heard what she thought about being made to lie on a pallet. As the girl who crouched on the floor beside Lagle shook her head, Ava said, "Very well. Have my old chamber prepared – the one where I was taken before I wed the prince – and see that she is moved there. She must be cared for as though she was the Queen herself, or…" Or Lagle would scream the very roof tiles off the place, Ava thought but didn't say. She swallowed. "Or you will answer to me," she finished instead.

"No, mistress, we cannot. Perhaps things are different where you are from, but here…we could never allow a girl of a lower caste taint the guest chambers of the very highest. She must stay here, as the Emperor commands." The maid shook her head furiously. "If the Emperor should hear of it, he will take all of our heads for allowing such a thing. Even if he does not take yours, he will make the prince punish you, for it is a husband's duty to discipline his wife. Better to let this girl die of her injuries than be injured yourself, mistress, for you surely would be. Prince Yun is as strong a warrior as any of his brothers."

Ava wished she could trade something, anything, for the courage to say that a girl's life was worth a little pain, but if her maids would have to die to give Lagle her golden bed, then a pallet wouldn't hurt her. Lagle would make her wishes and her position known the moment she woke.

"She wakes, mistress," the crouching girl said, nodding at Lagle.

Sure enough, Lagle's eyelids fluttered again as she screwed her face up. "My head hurts," she whimpered.

"Fetch her something for the pain," Ava ordered. "Quickly."

"Who are you?" Lagle asked, blinking. She gazed straight at Ava.

Before Ava could respond, one of the maids cut in, "This is your mistress, Princess Ava, wife to Prince Yun, eighth son of His Imperial

Highness, the Emperor himself. Show respect!"

Lagle lowered her gaze. "I seem to have forgotten. A thousand apologies, mistress. Have I overslept?"

This didn't sound like Lagle at all. "You took a blow to the head when your horse threw you," Ava said slowly, her heart sinking at Lagle's blank expression. "Don't you remember?"

Lagle shook her head. "No, mistress. I only feel fear when you speak of horses, and a desire to avoid them as much as I can. Yet you say I climbed upon one's back?"

Ava didn't know what to say. Could the bump to her head have scattered Lagle's wits and her memories, too? Bianca had told her tales of such things happening to soldiers in battle, but Ava had never imagined she'd see such a thing happen to Lagle, of all people.

"How dare you ask questions of your mistress! Show more respect!" a maid scolded.

Lagle cast her eyes down once more.

"Apologies, mistress. I forgot myself." She struggled to sit up. "Please forgive...augh!" Her voice died in an exclamation of pain and she flopped back to the pallet, lifeless, or seemingly so. She still drew breath, to Ava's relief.

"You should not be here, Princess," one of the maids said. "Permit me to take you to the pleasure gardens, where the other wives will be at this time of the day."

Ava nodded. There was little more she could do for Lagle until the girl woke again or regained her memory. Perhaps one of the other princesses would be willing to talk to her. It would be nice to have a friend, if such a thing were possible.

When they reached the garden, though, all thought of princesses or even people flew out of her head. Ava had never seen such a beautiful place. It was as lush as the forest she and Lagle had travelled through only yesterday, but far more beautiful. Flowers and scents assailed her on all sides, as she followed the path curving gently through what could only be paradise.

"That's Prince Chao's wife, Fang," the maid said softly, inclining her head. "She has not spoken since her wedding night, a year ago. He is the second son, and it is said that if Prince Gang, the crown prince, does not beget a son on his wife, Lan, that the Emperor will declare Chao his heir instead, for Fang has borne him a boy and she is already carrying a second, or so her maids say."

Ava tried not to stare at Princess Fang. Her silk robes draped around her in such a way that she could not tell if the woman was eight months pregnant or not carrying a child at all. Between her pale face and haunted eyes, Ava had the impression that the woman was more spirit than human. The shadows beneath the princess's eyes looked like bruises, instead of the evidence of sleepless nights. Perhaps they were both, Ava realised with alarm as she remembered what her maids had said in the bath house that morning.

A woman swathed in red silk moved slowly past, bent over with what Ava thought was age. Ava and her entourage halted to permit the dowager to pass.

It wasn't until the woman sank onto a bench, her attendants settling like a flock of birds around her, that Ava realised she wasn't elderly at all – the woman couldn't be more than twenty, if that. Her face screwed up in pain before she smoothed it into a blank look much like that of Princess Fang.

"I didn't think Princess Lan would be able to leave her bed for three days, at least," the maid said in a low voice.

"Is she ill?" Ava asked, taking a step toward her. If she couldn't help Lagle, perhaps she could be of service to someone else.

"If she were, she would not be here. The crown prince often speaks of setting her aside for a more fertile wife. As if three daughters in as many years is not fertile. No, her husband punishes her soundly after the birth of each girl. Half the palace hears him shout at her for failing to give him a son. The prince announced the birth of his daughter yesterday morning, vowing to beget a son that very day. Judging by how slowly she moves today, he's had her in his bed all day and all night, though the new babe is barely out of her belly. No wonder there was no salve left in the bath house this morning for you."

Ava gasped. What kind of prince would beat and bed his wife repeatedly for a day and a night? A monster, not a prince at all, she resolved angrily. "The men of this kingdom sound like monsters," Ava declared.

The maids gasped.

"Please, do not say that, mistress," one begged.

"They are merely men," the gossiping maid added. "They have wants and appetites that women must satisfy, without ever understanding why. All men want sons to send to war, to rule their lands and light incense in the shrines for them when they are gone. What else are women for, but to serve?"

This was not the way of things in the women's palace back home. True, the wives and concubines who lived there served her father, but not in such a way that interfered with their own pleasures. Occasionally a girl might not go horseriding for a few days after birth or after several nights with the King, but she would always say so with a sly smile, which the other wives and concubines shared. None of this haunted, pained expression shared by the princesses in this barbarian palace.

More than ever, Ava wanted to thank Prince Yun for his kindness last night. If not for him, she might be a quivering shadow of herself like the other girls.

"Will this suit you, mistress?" a maid asked, gesturing toward an empty bench.

Ava nodded, accepting their assistance to arrange her skirts as she settled onto her seat. While her maids gossiped about the other princesses in the palace, occasionally breaking off to bring Ava refreshments, Ava's mind wandered back to her home, and the Summer

Palace where Bianca had been taken. She wondered whether anyone missed her, and what they would say if they knew what was happening here. She thought about sending the Queen a note about her daughter's fall, but decided against it. Ava didn't want to fall afoul of the Queen's wrath ever again. Let Lagle write a letter to her mother when she recovered. Lagle wouldn't allow one of these barbarians to touch her, let alone wed her, and she'd want to go home. Leaving Ava alone among them. Ava wasn't sure whether she wanted that or not.

Now that she had flown from the harem, Ava wanted to see what this adventure had in store for her. A handsome prince for a husband might be just the start.

Twenty-One

Yun woke to birdsong. A screeching chorus that no man could withstand. He cracked open one eye and wished he hadn't, for the sunlight beat down on him mercilessly.

"I thought you would sleep all day," Mother's voice remarked.

He could not ignore the Empress.

Yun levered himself up into a sitting position, rolling his shoulders to rid them of stiffness. He should not have slept on a bench in his mother's private garden. Yet where else in the palace could he find peace?

"Did you make a poor choice of wife?" Mother asked.

Yun wanted to argue that both she and his father had pushed him into the marriage, but he knew that the decision had still been his own. He thought of the lovely Princess Ava, probably still asleep in his bed.

"No." He sighed. "She is lovely and obedient and everything I could want. A worthy wife, in all the ways I could name. I simply could not sleep, so I walked the walls for a while, and then I think I came here." He frowned. "I did not mean to fall asleep."

Mother laughed softly. "Your father came here looking for you, but I told him not to wake you. He made me promise to remind you that it is her duty to bear sons, and yours to beget them."

More fools for the court, to take after their father, Yun thought sadly but didn't say. With his seven older brothers, his sons would never be heirs to his father's throne.

"You may rest a little here, first, though," Mother continued. "I will send for some food and drink. Is there something you wish to ask me?"

For a moment, Yun considered confessing last night's subterfuge to his mother. But he banished the idea as quickly as it had come. No, he could tell no one. There were few secrets in the palace, and anything said aloud could be overheard.

He rose and headed for the cage of birds. A flurry of bright wings warned him he had come too close for the comfort of some. Did Ava long to flee from him, too?

Amid the bright parrots and orioles, there was a plain-looking bird in brown and white. "Mother, what is that bird? I don't think I've seen it before."

The Empress approached. "I thought you'd ask me questions about women, or pleasing your wife, not birds. If you mean my newest pet, she is a lark. One of your brothers brought her back for me from the Horse People's lands, thinking I might enjoy her song. But she has not sung yet." Mother stared intently at the bird. "Perhaps she is not yet comfortable in her new home. Or maybe her heart does not hold enough joy to raise her voice in song."

"It is a hard thing to abandon the life you knew, and make your home anew," Yun said slowly, thinking of Ava. Her courage was greater than even he'd known. What, and who, had she left behind?

Refreshments arrived, and he made small talk with his mother for as long as politeness required. Yet his restless mind wandered, from Ava to the birds before darting back to Ava again.

"Where is Ava, Mother?" he asked suddenly.

She laughed. "I'm surprised it's taken you so long to ask. She is in the pleasure garden, with the other princesses."

Yun's heart sank. The other princesses were his brothers' wives. If they talked to her, they were bound to tell her about his brothers. Girls gossiped, and they would welcome another who was their equal. Even now, they could be frightening her with stories of their wedding nights, or of any night since, knowing his brothers and their tastes.

If she suspected him of being like his brothers, she would run screaming at the sight of him, he was sure of it.

Then he would be forced to give up all hope of ever having a willing wife.

No, he did not want that. He wanted her, one day, even if that day was far into the future.

One day he would hear his lovely lark sing.

Yun bade his mother farewell and headed off to find his wife.

Twenty-Two

What sounded like a smothered scream jolted Ava out of her daydream about swimming with Bianca at the Summer Palace. Ava scanned the garden, just in time to see Princess Lan fall off her chair, to the consternation of her attendants. Together, they carried her inside the palace.

Ava prepared to return to her thoughts, when another sound caught her attention – this time, a male voice.

"Have you seen her?" the man asked.

Princess Fang dropped to her knees on the grass, extending her hand in Ava's direction.

The man turned and a grin lit his face. "There's my little wife! My illustrious father reminded me that a marriage is not successful without sons, so it's off to bed for you. I hope you're well rested after last night, for there'll be very little sleep for you tonight, either."

Behind him, Princess Fang fainted.

Prince Yun didn't seem to notice as he marched across the grass toward Ava, beckoning imperiously. "Come along, bed! The Emperor commands it!"

Numbly, Ava obeyed his summons, following him on leaden feet back into the cold darkness of the palace.

He led her to the bedroom they'd shared after the wedding ceremony, and waited for her to enter before closing the door firmly behind her. Then he set his back to the oak door and just grinned.

Silence stretched for a long moment before Ava ventured, "Would you like me to disrobe for you, Your Highness?"

His eyes burned with desire, answering for him.

Swallowing, Ava fumbled with the ties of her gown.

His large hand closed over both of hers, making undressing impossible. Prince Yun's eyes softened as they met hers. "My body would have me say yes, and make you a proper, dutiful wife, like it wanted to do last night." He sighed. "But my spirit refuses, insisting that you are more than a simple vessel to hold children."

Remembering the words of her gossiping maids in the garden, Ava said, "It seems that is all your people believe women are for." She winced at the accusation in her tone.

Yun clapped his hands. "So you have heard the other princesses' stories, yet you are not afraid. There is the spirit I saw yesterday! Such courage."

Ava couldn't help it. She laughed. "I have no courage, Your Highness. What you mistake for courage is pure terror, stopping me from running away from what frightens me, as a sensible person should."

Yun shook his head. "No. I saw terror, too, but I saw more courage in you yesterday than on a battlefield full of men. You sat there, on your knees in his throne room, and defied the Emperor himself to his face. I couldn't let my brothers break such a spirit. You are a treasure. And so, here we are. Keep your clothes on, if you wish. Amuse yourself as you please. I have a poem that burns to be released, if I have but the wit to write it." He headed for the table in the corner of the room by the window, and searched among the papers that covered it until he unearthed a brush.

Ava didn't know what to do. "So you don't want me, Your Highness?" The words came out sounding forlorn.

"Weren't you listening to a word I said?" he asked without looking up.

"I listened, but I still don't understand."

He sighed. "Did you not hear me call you a

treasure?"

"Yes, but –"

"What does one normally do with treasures?" he asked calmly.

"Keep them safe," Ava whispered. "Like you kept me safe from your brothers by marrying me yesterday."

"And from me," he added.

"But the...but they say you are different to your brothers. Not like them," Ava began, fearful all over again. If he never bedded her, she'd never bear him a son. If there were no sons, the Emperor would order him to punish her and...Ava shivered at the thought of being beaten so badly that she hobbled around like Princess Lan or that she might faint at the sound of a man's voice, like Princess Fang.

He laughed softly. "Barely here a day and you already know the palace gossip. If your father sent you here as a spy, we are all doomed."

"My father didn't – "

He hushed her. "No need to protest,

Princess. No one can feign terror like you showed yesterday. My father already believes you to be a spy, and whether you are or not, he will not allow you to get a message out to your father, no matter what you discover. Other than that, you are my wife, entitled to all the honour and privilege due to a princess in the palace. Enjoy it. I doubt many of the others do." He dipped his brush in a jar of ink and began to write.

So he had seen the state of the other princesses, and still done nothing. "When will you break me like your brothers have done with their wives?"

Yun set his brush down. "I am not my brothers."

Ava wet her lips. "But you are still a man, and I am your wife. Those poor girls in the garden – when will that be my fate? I deserve to know."

He rose and strode toward her until barely a breath separated them. "What if I say now? What if I tell you to take off your clothes, lie on the bed and spread your legs, like a good wife?"

Ava's hands went to untie her lacings once more. "Then I will be a good wife, like I should."

Again, Yun stopped her. "Enough with the undressing! I will not have an unwilling wife!"

"I married you willingly," Ava said steadily. "And I am willing to give my body to you, to do with as you wish, just as I was last night."

"That wasn't willing! That was grudging."

Ava took a deep breath to steady herself. She wanted to give up, but something within her wouldn't let her. "I am willing."

"No, you're not. Willing is when you want me so much, you would search through the palace to find me, drag me back to your bedchamber, tear off my clothes, and have your way with me." Yun's eyes were dark and unreadable. "Are you willing to do all of those things?"

Ava couldn't seem to close her mouth. Did women really do such things? She'd heard stories in the harem and Bianca told more tales than most. Empresses who had kept harems of men solely for their pleasure. Women who had their own desires and needs and destinies, who…

"You look lost."

Yun's amused words drew Ava out of her dream. "Only lost in thought, Your Highness," she said. "Especially as you searched for me, found me, brought me back here and…and…it would be a shame to tear such lovely clothes."

Yun tilted her chin up so her eyes met his. "There are plenty more in the palace. If you want me in your bed, say so, and you shall have me."

As Ava looked into his eyes, she felt like she'd swallowed a snake that now writhed in her belly. There was something about this man that made her want to say yes. After all, Prince Yun was not like his brothers.

The image of the two broken princesses in the garden popped into Ava's mind. If a prince could do such a thing to his wife...

Yun moved away. "Let me know if you change your mind. I'll have to share your bed for the first month of marriage, as custom demands, but I won't touch you unless you ask me. You may retire when you please. I will continue writing poetry while I still have light."

He returned to the table and his papers.

Ava sat on the edge of the bed, suddenly exhausted by the exchange. Would she ever be willing in the way he said? Was it worth a chance to find out if the tales were true, and a woman could take pleasure in her marriage bed? Could she, with Yun?

A man she barely knew, Ava scoffed, as she often had to Bianca when her sister had told her tales of couples falling madly in love on their first meeting. Bianca insisted such a thing was true, but Ava had her doubts. What happened in tales rarely occurred in real life. If she trusted Yun, perhaps she would not mind so much when he touched her. To trust him she must know him better.

"I have heard that poetry speaks of the writer's spirit," Ava said slowly. "May I read some of yours?"

"Absolutely not," Yun replied.

Defeated, Ava readied herself for sleep. When she had removed all her clothing except her shift, she climbed beneath the blankets and tried to sleep, but rest eluded her. Her thoughts swirled too fast.

"Why not?" Ava asked finally.

Yun turned to stare at her. "What?"

Ava had a strong desire to stay silent, but she'd been brave enough to ask once, and a tiny whisper of courage still remained. "Why won't you let me read your poetry?" she asked.

"Because I won't let anyone read it. It's not good enough to be shown to anyone."

Ava wasn't sure what to reply to that. "One day, I would like to read it," she said finally.

"Then you will be the first."

Yun returned to his work, and Ava decided not to disturb him further. She could ask him again later. After all, they were married now, and would be sharing a bed for a month. Surely he'd give in to her eventually.

Twenty-Three

Yun tried to concentrate on the page before him. With all his might, he strove to conjure up the image of a noble battle, an army victorious. He'd have settled for the bloody battlefield, strewn with corpses. Yet all he could see in his mind's eye was her hands, fluttering at her breast as she offered to unlace her dress.

Willing, yet wishing she could fly free. Far from fearless, for she knew about his brothers and their wives, though she did not fear him.

Laughter like chattering parrots as she described her terror.

What sort of woman laughed in the face of her own fear?

If he touched her breast, would her heart flutter beneath his fingers?

With trepidation, he lifted his brush and wrote:

My love is a bird

Bright of eye with airy wing

Fluttering high with my heart

Teaching it to sing

The moment the words were on the paper, he wanted to screw it up and throw it across the room. He would not sing, not if he couldn't compose something about his brothers' victory.

"I have heard that poetry speaks of the writer's spirit."

Yun stared at her. Why was she still awake? Had she watched him write words about her?

A faint blush coloured her cheeks. "May I read some of yours?" she continued.

Show her his feeble love poem? Then she truly would know him for a fool.

"Absolutely not," he said firmly, trying to sound as frightening as his father. If she was the obedient wife she claimed to be, she would not push further.

Yun waited, every muscle held in taut expectation as he prepared to defend his piece of paper from her sight, but she merely moved past him to lay her clothes on the chest at the end of the bed. The shift she left on was too large for her tiny frame, drifting around her like cloud, or mist, letting him see curving details that tantalised him before they disappeared beneath the linen veil.

His brush moved almost of its own accord over the page:

My love is a dream

Clothed in caressing mist

Even in silence

Her lips beg to be kissed.

"Why not?" she asked softly.

Yun dropped his brush. "What?"

"Why won't you let me read your poetry?" she asked.

Because it is about you, he thought but could not say. Because it's not good enough. And it never would be. Yun stammered an excuse, but she didn't seem to be listening. She just regarded him, dark eyes deep with thoughts she did not share.

His thoughts whispered unbidden:

My love is a mystery

I long to uncover

Wrapping her in my arms

She chooses me as her lover.

Her voice was soft, tentative, like she feared to frighten him. "One day, I would like to read it." Her dark eyes reflected her sincerity, but they also implored.

By the ancestors, when she looked at him like that, he could deny her nothing. "Then you will be the first," he promised. Trying to remember the words of those last few lines, Yun lifted his brush. To his dismay, the ink had smeared across the page, leaving most of it unreadable.

He pulled out a fresh piece of parchment and dipped the brush into the ink once more. The smooth strokes of the brush were almost hypnotic as he wrote the words out again, before adding the final lines. He blew on the page gently to dry it, not willing to bury his precious poem in sand.

It also gave him an excuse to delay showing her. Would she like it, or think him a fool? He wasn't a poet, not truly. He only had to pull out a single scroll bearing the immortal words of Li Yu – perhaps his poem about the Heavenly Woman. Li's words conjured her up perfectly, with the love he felt for his empress, for he was both wise emperor and skilled poet.

Neither of which Yun would ever be.

Yun sighed. The ink was dry – he could delay no longer. Holding the scroll before him as his shield, he turned to face Ava. Let her think of him as she would.

Her glossy hair shimmered like a cloud on the pillow, drawing his attention to the feathers of her dark lashes against her cheek as she slept. He didn't want to wake her. Not for something as inconsequential as his poem.

Yet he couldn't resist approaching for a closer look at his sleeping wife. Heedless of where he stepped, Yun brushed against her shed clothes, sending them sliding to the floor. He bent to retrieve them, and was struck by the wondrous fragrance emanating from the silk. He buried his face in the fabric and inhaled like a drowning man drawing his first gasping breath.

Ava. If her clothes smelled so lovely, what bliss it would be to feel her silken skin against his, instead of just her discarded garments? Stronger, more heady, and much harder to resist, he was certain.

He forced himself to stay back, keeping his distance from the bed where she slept. He gripped the screen by the wall, the silvery pearl-shell smooth under his fingers. Would she feel this smooth? Only not so hard and cold. Softer and warmer and…

The folding screen clacked shut, nearly making him fall over.

Yun swore. If Ava opened her eyes now, she would see him as he truly was – a bumbling fool.

Luckily, her eyes remained fast shut. One day, perhaps they would regard him with love.

In the meantime, he would attempt to write something better. Poor poetry was hardly likely to win this lady's heart.

Twenty-Four

When her maids were done dressing her the following day, Ava asked to see Lagle again. The palace was too quiet for her sister to have recovered, and she worried about what would happen to her if Lagle died. The Queen had a long reach, and Ava shivered at the thought of what the Queen might do to her here.

After considerable hesitation, the girls led her back to the room where she'd first seen Lagle, only to find it empty.

Ava stared down at the thin pallet, hope

rising in her breast. "So she is recovered, and she has been moved to a better chamber?" she asked eagerly.

The maids held a whispered conference.

Finally, one ventured, "We do not know, mistress."

"Find out, then," Ava snapped, startling herself with her imperious tone. She opened her mouth to apologise for the curt order.

"Yes, mistress," the maids chorused.

One of them added, "Would you like to go to the gardens now, mistress?"

Ava agreed – what else did she have to do here? – and followed them to the spot where she'd spent most of the previous day.

Today, she was restless, with no desire to sit around all day long until Yun came to frighten all the other wives and fetch her again. Besides, she'd only seen two of them yesterday – with seven other sons, that made at least five more wives she hadn't yet met. They couldn't all be quivering wrecks.

So Ava strolled through the gardens,

listening to her maids relate the goings-on inside the palace as Ava tried to spot the other wives. One of them was asleep on a bench, while one of her attendants fanned flying insects away from her face. Another had actually climbed partway up a tree, so that she sat on a broad branch above Ava's head. Her attendants knelt on the grass below their mistress's tree, quietly sewing.

None of the princesses looked up as Ava passed, though their attendants shot her a curious glance or two. It was like being invisible.

"Why won't they look at me?" Ava blurted out, until realisation dawned. "Never mind, I know."

She was the newest wife of the youngest son. A nobody. The lowest ranking woman in the harem, just as she had been at home. Bianca was wrong. Nothing ever changed for Ava.

"I beg your pardon, mistress. What did you say?" a maid asked.

"Nothing," Ava replied, waving away her initial concerns. "I answered my own question. The other wives won't look at me or speak to me because I am beneath them. I am the wife of the youngest son."

The maids gasped.

"Oh, no, mistress," one of them said. "They were high ranking ladies in the court before they married and became the princes' wives. You were born a princess. They lower their gazes in respect for your high rank. They would not dare speak first to a princess of royal blood. It is a wonder that Prince Gang did not set aside Lan so that he might marry you instead. If Prince Yun hadn't taken a fancy to you and insisted on marrying you immediately…but the Empress is fond of her youngest son. Perhaps the Emperor chose to honour him to please the Empress when he gave you to him."

Ava opened her mouth to say she was no prize, but words failed her. Perhaps things were different at this foreign court, after all.

Twenty-Five

"Is there good news, sir?"

Yun dragged his thoughts away from his search for the right words to describe Ava's voice. "Hmm?"

The guardsman coughed. "Beg pardon, Your Highness. But seeing as you're whistling so cheerfully and all, I thought you might have heard some good news."

He'd been whistling? Yun couldn't remember the last time he'd done that. But he couldn't think of any news, except... "I have a new wife," Yun said. He supposed that was news.

"I'd heard, sir. Congratulations. We heard she was some sort of barbarian princess. One of the Horse People." Though only his eyes were visible, his expression was uncomfortable. "Is it true that she's a witch, sir?"

She'd bewitched him, in ways Yun hadn't thought possible. Yet he found himself shaking his head. "She is the loveliest woman I ever beheld. Sweet and obedient and…" And what? He knew very little about her, aside from her courage in the face of her fears. But fearlessness was not something a man normally praised in his wife. The clouds shifted, pouring sunlight down on the battlements. It warmed him like…like her request to see his poetry, though he had yet to show her. He'd managed to avoid it so far, but perhaps tonight… "She can make sunlight sing," he finished.

The guardsman coughed again. "I've never

heard it sing. Sounds like magic to me, sir, if you don't mind me saying."

But it wasn't. It was just...Ava. "Are you married?"

"No, sir."

"Ever been in love?"

"I love my mother and my father, and my family, sir."

Yun laughed softly. "I mean with a girl. So in love with a girl, your heart would burst if she married another man?"

"I don't think so, sir."

Yun clapped the man on the shoulder. "Then consider yourself fortunate. For love can create magic so powerful, I don't believe even a witch could break the spell. When such a spell is cast on you, then we can raise a drink together and toast the magic of love."

"It would be an honour, Your Highness."

It wasn't until the guardsman was gone that Yun realised he hadn't even asked the man's name. So caught up in his thoughts of Ava...

Tonight he would show her his work, Yun

vowed. Good or bad, it would at least tell her the depth of his feelings for her. Perhaps they might even share a kiss, a prelude to something more…

He walked the walls as though wings were attached to his feet. The sunlight sparkled on the river particularly prettily today. Shun the gooseherd had a new assistant this morning, who was quite the dullard, to hear him shout at her. But the girl had been foisted on him by his superiors, so he was stuck with her, or so he said.

Yun watched, bemused. Who would give a girl to the gooseherd?

But as the girl and her hissing flock passed beneath the wall, Yun felt a jolt of recognition. She wasn't just any girl. She was Ava's maid, the girl he'd carried into the palace on the day they arrived. It was madness to make a lady's maid into a bird herder.

This was his father's doing, Yun decided. He'd talked of separating Ava from her maid, and this was how he'd accomplished it. Sheer foolishness, is what it was.

Yun descended to the courtyard and marched purposefully toward the throne room. Ava was no danger to them, he was certain of it. Where was the harm in letting her see a familiar face every day on one of the maids who helped her dress? He would speak to his father and secure the services of the new goose girl. Without her geese.

An hour later, Yun emerged from the throne room, his head full of his father's words, but he still did not have the goose girl. His father insisted she must stay where she was, for her own good, if it was to be believed, for she had some sort of brain fever, the physicians said, and she must be kept away from other people lest the disease spread.

Yun shook his head. He didn't understand it. Who had ever heard of a disease that attacked the mind? Unless this madness had infected the physicians, too…

"Your Highness!"

Yun slowed to a stop. "Yes?"

The servant halted, breathing hard. She wore silk, marking her as a lady-in-waiting to someone of importance. Yun didn't recognise her, but then he didn't know all of his mother's servants. And who else would send for him?

"Your Highness, you are needed in the pleasure garden. Your wife has gone mad!"

No. Not Ava. Yun broke into a run.

Twenty-Six

A week passed, each day much the same as the others. Every night she shared a bed with Prince Yun, who said little to her and didn't touch her at all. Each morning, the maids would serve her breakfast and help her bathe and dress before accompanying her to the pleasure garden for another day of sharing palace gossip.

Mostly, Ava just let their voices wash over her, drowsing in the sweet-scented air like the other wives did. Yet after a week, the endless stream of stories began to irritate her.

"I don't care whose wife is sleeping with which official in order to get her daughter on the list of potential brides for the crown prince!" Ava burst out. "How can you know so much about who shares whose bed when you can't tell me where Lagle is!"

The maids babbled their apologies, but today Ava would have none of it. Whenever she had been this frustrated in the women's palace, Bianca had dragged her to the stables. A day spent with the horses always helped.

"Have my horse saddled. I wish to ride," Ava said, wondering for the first time where the palace ponies were kept. None of the other wives seemed to want to do more than sit and stare into space in the garden, but that only made Ava feel useless.

One of her maids hurried away to relay her order to the grooms, while the others ushered her back to her chambers to change into suitable riding clothes. The skirt of the robe she wore today was wrapped so closely around her legs that Ava struggled to take more than the tiniest steps. Attempting to mount a horse would show a scandalous amount of her legs, or rip the fine silk asunder, neither of which Ava wanted. Especially if Lagle discovered Ava had destroyed her favourite new gown, as surely this must be.

More appropriately attired, Ava returned to the garden to wait for her horse. She didn't have to wait long – her breathless maid hurried across the grass, dropped to her knees and said, "Mistress, I asked for your horse, but the grooms say it's no longer in the stables. It's gone."

A red haze misted Ava's vision. "First Lagle, now my horse! Can you find nothing in this palace? What will I do when you lose my clothes as well? Go naked?"

Amid exclamations of horror and another round of apologies, one maid's voice quavered, "But you did not bring any clothing, mistress. The Emperor commanded that we only bring you new gowns fit for a princess in the

Emperor's palace. If we were to lose these, the imperial tailors would only make more for you."

Ava's mouth gaped. She wasn't wearing Lagle's clothes after all? Her own clothes had been in the saddlebags strapped to her own horse, so Ava knew her things had arrived with her. One of the gowns had been a gift from Bianca, embroidered by her own hand. And the cup Militsa had given her as a parting gift had been among her things. Was all she owned to be lost in this enormous, heartless palace?

Her maids cowered as Ava began to shout in earnest, venting her frustration at the top of her lungs to the very trees themselves, for it felt like no one else was listening.

"So have you truly gone mad?" a loud male voice interrupted.

Ava whirled.

Yun stood before her with his arms folded, an amused look on his face. "One of Princess Lan's attendants told me that my wife had gone mad and I had best deal with her before my father heard about it. I suspect it's too late for that. Half the palace has heard you, and that half is terrified." He gestured around the garden.

Only now did Ava realise the effect of her outburst. Lan and Fang had curled up on their benches, their hands over their ears, oblivious to the attempts of their attendants to calm them, and the other wives looked almost as frightened.

"I only wanted to know where Lagle and my horse were. And my things," Ava said. "No one will tell me."

"You never asked me," Yun said.

"No, I didn't," she said slowly. "Do you know where they are?"

He grasped her arm, firmly but without hurting her. "Come, I'll show you."

Willingly, Ava walked with him through the passageways of the palace, trying not to hold her breath. If she could just be sure Lagle was safe and she found the gifts from her family, it would be all right. Her horse and her clothes were nothing special. Not like the gowns packed for Lagle, fit for a queen, or Falada, the magnificent warhorse who had seemed intelligent enough to make his wishes known.

Ava barely managed to keep up with Yun as he took the stairs two at a time, to a level of the palace Ava was sure she hadn't seen before. Surely she had to be at the very top of the palace, she thought as she struggled to catch her breath. No one would keep horses up here. Falada would break down the door of his stall rather than be stabled so high.

"Here." Yun pulled Ava out onto a balcony where the overhanging roof hid them in its shadows. "There's your maid."

Ava scarcely recognised Lagle as the girl garbed in brown like a nun. Her clothes certainly weren't silk, for Lagle paused to itch a spot where the rough fabric evidently troubled her.

Ava started to ask why her sister was dressed so poorly, when a deafening cacophony filled the air. The honking of what appeared to be a hundred geese, which flapped and waddled around Lagle's feet, drowned out anything Ava could say.

A man emerged from among the geese, aiming a cuff at Lagle's head. Ava gasped at the thought of him striking her, but Lagle ducked aside so the blow never landed. Almost as if she'd had practice. She flapped her hands like wings at her sides, urging the geese out the gate. The birds obeyed her, rushing to put themselves between the man and Lagle.

"Who is that man?" Ava asked.

"Shun, keeper of the royal geese," Yun said. "He's the only one who was willing to take on a girl whose head is addled, but I think he heartily regrets agreeing to it."

"Addled? Her head is addled?" Ava repeated. The Queen would never forgive her if Lagle didn't recover. She would...

"When she seemed recovered, my father ordered her put to work, but not for you. He still thinks you're a spy. He sent her to the kitchens, but she burned the rice and has no skills with a knife when she was set to peeling the vegetables. They sent her to the laundry, but she ruined one of my mother's favourite gowns, so she was sent back. She cannot remember how to do anything, it seems. She can't sing or sew or cook or wash, and my father ordered one of his guards to execute her, for there is no place in the palace for a servant who has forgotten how to serve. She fell to her knees in the courtyard, begging to be allowed to live, when Shun came in with the geese. The whole great honking lot of them. The birds attacked the guards, the way geese do, and it was chaos for some time until she shouted at the birds to be silent. They did, so my father gave her to Shun to be his assistant. She doesn't even remember her name, so they all just call her the goose girl, for she's the only one who can command the geese."

"What did Lagle say about it?" Ava asked.

Yun shrugged. "I don't know. Thanked my father and the ancestors for sparing her, I suppose, and hurried off to tend the geese before he changed his mind." He nodded at Lagle. "This is as close as you'll get to her. You won't be allowed to speak to her, or give her any messages to take out of the palace. As for your horse…"

Lagle had stopped at the gates. She wiped something from her hair and looked up.

Ava gagged. Someone had suspended Falada's head from the gate. Recently, too, for blood still dripped from it – that's what Lagle had wiped off her hair.

"Why?" Ava choked out. "Why kill a perfectly good horse and do that to him?"

"That horse injured three grooms before one of my guards took his head," Yun said. "Quite uncontrollable. Didn't you say he threw your maid and nearly broke her head?"

"Yes, but…" Ava wanted to say that Lagle had been a poor rider, goading him into it. "He was spooked," she said instead.

"Well, he's a horse spirit now, and maybe he can do some good to fix the damage he did. The healers swear the best way to cure her head is to hang up the horse's head until his spirit restores her mind. I didn't quite understand the details – they spoke of humours and elements and all manner of things that are beyond the knowledge of a simple poet," Yun said.

"Not just a poet," Ava said. "A prince and a soldier, too."

"And a husband, who has his duty to perform," Yun said gravely. "Do you know the cure for a wilful wife, who asks too many questions and shouts when women should be silent?"

Ava shook her head, though she suspected she knew the answer.

"A properly masterful husband, who shows her where her place is. And yours is in bed, wife!" Yun said gleefully as he took her arm once more and escorted her back to his chambers.

Where he would abandon her to spend all evening on his poetry again, as he had every other night she spent with him, Ava knew. For all his talk of bedding her, this was the first time he'd laid a hand on her all week, and he released her the moment they were alone.

It wasn't until much later that night that Ava remembered her cup, and by then, Yun was asleep in the bed beside her, snoring softly in the dark. She hadn't the heart to wake him, so she resolved to ask in the morning. Nothing seemed to change here, so one night couldn't make a difference, surely.

Or so Ava thought.

Twenty-Seven

The goose girl felt something drip onto her face. She glanced up, expecting rain, but all she saw was the red-painted gate with a horse head hanging beneath it. As she watched, a large drop of blood detached from the head and splattered to the cobbles by her feet. Something landed in her hair and when she touched it, her fingers came away red. Nothing made sense to the goose girl; this least of all.

Herding geese, hanging horses from gates, wearing a scratchy brown robe, sleeping on a straw pallet that she was certain contained fleas…she longed for a hot bath, big enough to immerse herself in to scrub off all the filth. The thought was gone as quickly as it had come, for how would a peasant girl who tended to geese ever receive the luxury of a hot bath? She bathed with a cloth and a jug of water when she could. If she wanted to bathe her whole body at once, she had best take a dip in the river.

A gobbet of flesh landed on her shoulder, staining her robe red before she could shake it off. A dip with her clothes on, the goose girl promised herself, so that she might wash her robe along with herself. Best to find a private spot, where Shun couldn't watch her. She'd already caught him leering at her in the servants' sleeping chamber, when she washed, and he hadn't been the only man who did. The only thing that kept their hands off her was the whispered rumours of her being a foreign witch.

The goose girl had almost laughed when she

heard it – how could a girl who couldn't remember her own name be a powerful witch, capable of casting spells? Yet they saw the way the geese obeyed her and said it was witchcraft. One night, one of them would grow bold enough to do more than watch, though, and she knew she had no spell to stop him.

Best to bathe in the river, then, the goose girl resolved, chivvying her charges through the gate, toward the lake where they spent their days. Like every other day she could remember, the goose girl followed the river, then walked along the bank of the canal that led to the lake. When the lake was full, it emptied out into a little stream that rejoined the river a half mile downstream, but the hot spring days had drunk the lake water until the water level had dropped so much that the stream ran dry.

The goose girl shooed her birds into the lake, then waited for Shun to catch up. He came huffing and puffing down the hill, then flopped down under a tree. He drank deeply from the water bottle he kept tied to his belt, then threw it at the goose girl. "I'm empty. Fetch me a drink, girl."

"From the lake?" she asked. Surely it would have been easier for him to sit beside the lake, where he could drink as much as he pleased, instead of sitting under a tree ten yards away.

"Of course not, dolt. The geese and the city foul the lake so it's not safe to drink. Fill my bottle in the river."

The goose girl snatched up the bottle, darting into the dry stream bed. She jumped down the steps that had once been a pretty waterfall, following the sound of running water to the river. She found where the stream fed the river, then turned upstream. The river curved a little to go around a massive tree, and she had to fight her way through underbrush to reach the bank on the other side of the tree. When she did, she drew in a breath.

The pool before her was perfect. The tree had dammed part of the river to create a pool that had none of the river's turbulence, yet it looked deep enough for the goose girl's longed-for bath. Dappled sunlight glinted on the pool's surface, enticing her in.

First, she opened the water bottle and filled it in the pool, before jamming the stopper into the neck of the bottle. She set the bottle between two tree roots, half immersed in the pool, to keep the contents cool. The remains of a tiny broken glass bottle were caught between the roots, but the goose girl paid it no heed. Now, her time was her own.

The goose girl had no patience for getting in slowly. She simply stepped in and sank, letting the water close over her head before realising the pool was deeper than the expected. She thrashed to the surface, relieved to find it wasn't far.

Coughing and spluttering, she stayed at the surface until she had caught her breath once more, before she slipped out of her hated robe. She scrubbed it against a tree root, rinsing it until she could no longer see the blood. Then, she draped it over a branch, hoping it would dry while she washed herself.

But washing was thirsty work. The goose girl shifted to where the river fed her pool, and cupped her hands for a drink. The water was cool in her hands, but the first sip burned her tongue. Nevertheless, she drank more, sucking the drops from her fingers until they were dry.

A princess should drink from her golden cup, not her hands, her mother's voice insisted. A princess bathed only in perfumed water, brought to her by her many servants.

Knowledge blossomed in the goose girl's head.

"Where's my drink, girl?" an irate male voice demanded. Shun's head appeared over the underbrush.

"Fetch it yourself," Lagle told the fowl keeper. Princesses did not serve peasants.

"If I have to drag you out of there, I'll box your ears, girl," he threatened. "I'm not scared of no witch."

Witch. Lagle tasted the word, feeling it curl around her tongue as she drank more of the river water. It burned her throat like the finest wine. "You should be scared," she purred, stepping out of the pool. Water cascaded down her naked body, shimmering in the sunlight. "I am the most powerful witch your pitiful kingdom has ever seen. I will ensorcel your king and eat his heart."

"I'll tell the guards you said that!" Shun said, backing away.

"Do. Tell them to bring me robes fit for a queen when they come for me. I will wear nothing but silk now," Lagle said, lifting her cupped hand over her head so that more of the enchanted water trickled into her mouth. The more she drank, the more powerful she felt. "Have them deliver me to the king."

Shun disappeared out of sight.

"You forgot your water bottle!" she called, but received no answer. "My water bottle now," she said to herself, as the enchanted water within her began to whisper what she needed to do to become a queen.

Lagle listened.

Twenty Eight

Constant worry about what the Queen would do to her nagged at Ava's mind until she could scarcely sleep. In the garden the next day, she drowsed while her maids gossiped, until she heard a voice urgently calling her name.

"Princess Ava, you are summoned to the throne room."

Ava opened her eyes to find two guards before her. She bit her lip, forcing away the memories of the guards who'd escorted her back to the harem in her father's palace, and rose. She had to almost run to keep up with the two soldiers whose strides were much longer than hers, and her racing heart wasn't helped by the panic that engulfed her.

Had the Queen discovered Lagle's injury and Ava's marriage already? Ava couldn't think of any other reason why she would be summoned to the throne room, unless the Queen or someone from her father's court was here to punish her. Unless the Emperor knew that she and Yun hadn't consummated their marriage.

Ava's feet felt heavier with each step. She didn't want to face whatever awaited her, but if she ran, where would she go? It was all very well to think brave fishy thoughts, but it was another thing entirely to take a leap into the unknown. Perhaps the Emperor wished to apologise to her for believing her to be a spy.

The guards escorted her to the foot of the Emperor's dais, where she dropped into a deep curtsey before she could be commanded to do so.

"There's the lying, traitorous slut," Lagle said.

Ava gasped, raising her head to see Lagle seated beside the Emperor on the throne normally occupied by the Empress, who was nowhere to be seen.

"Bow before royalty, peasant!" Lagle ordered.

Ava couldn't help it. She smiled. "You are well, sister," she said. "Thank the ancestors that you have recovered."

"You are no family of mine!" Lagle stormed. "Tell the king what you really are. Tell him you are my insubordinate maid who turned traitor the moment my guards were out of sight, making my horse throw me off then switching clothes with me while I was unconscious so that the king would believe you were his bride, and not me. Tell him how you stole my rightful husband, pretending to be a princess, when you were really sent here as my maid to serve me. Tell him why you're here!"

Tears sprang to Ava's eyes, but she

struggled to speak before her throat choked up. "I'm here to seek peace between my father and the Emperor through a marriage alliance between his family and mine. When you fell off your horse, I lifted you back on and led you here, making sure you were cared for before I even saw the Emperor. I did…what had to be done. As my father's daughter." She swallowed. "I am a princess, the same as you."

"You are not the same as me," Lagle spat. "Guards! Execute her!"

A hand grasped Ava's arm, dragging her to her feet. She opened her mouth to scream, only to discover that the hand belonged to Yun.

"A wife's punishment is her husband's duty," Yun said dully. "Princess Ava is my wife, and no one shall touch her but me."

He yanked Ava's arm, dragging her out of the throne room. Too late, she realised that he was enveloped in a faint red glow – a curse, and one Ava recognised. She scanned the throne room, seeing the same glow emanate from Lagle, the Emperor, and the younger crowned men who shared the dais. Yun's seven brothers, she assumed. All under the same spell.

The curse hummed with malevolence as Yun dragged her out the door, heedless of how much he hurt her. This wasn't like him – the man who'd sworn not to touch her without her asking him to. Ava tried to concentrate on the curse to distract herself from the pain.

Red, yes, and filled with hate, it was a sort of seduction curse, which drew all men to one woman, slaves to her every wish. Lagle had somehow enslaved Yun, his father and his brothers with this curse. Ava had to break it or she would die, she knew. She cast her mind deeper into the magic, looking for the key to break the curse.

She gasped when she found it, for the solution was so simple.

But would it work?

Twenty-Nine

Punish your wives for being unfaithful, the witch's voice whispered in Yun's head. Put your children to death for being bastards. Then return to me and battle with your brothers, for the victor will have me and the throne.

Over and over, the words repeated, as he tried to shake them out of his head. He felt the compulsion to obey, but the thought of a woman as spoils of war turned his stomach.

And Ava…Ava…he took one look at her and the witch's voice rose in volume, drowning out Ava's sweet tones. A wife who had not yet given him children because he had not given them to her. The throne was not his. Never would be his. Leave it for his brothers to fight over.

Punish your wife! The witch's voice rose to a shriek in his head.

Yun took Ava's arm and repeated the witch's words. He would punish his wife.

Who had never done anything wrong. Staring into her eyes, he knew this with a certainty he could not deny.

Help her to fly. Open the gate.

In his head, Ava stood in the horse pen in his brothers' war camp. But where the other girls cowered in the corner, she stood tall. Reached down of her own accord and opened the gate.

"Better to fly than die," she said, echoing his own words. "I choose to be free. You must choose, too."

"I serve the Emperor's throne, and I will never be free," Yun told her. "But I will protect you, so that you may be."

Her fingers stroked his cheeks, her dark eyes burning with a passion Yun had never seen before. Her lips were warm and sweet, everything he had imagined she might be, and more. He pulled her close, determined to kiss her properly. To show her the depths of his passion. How much he longed for her, wanted no one else but her.

She let out a little sigh, parting her lips to tease him with her tongue.

No woman had ever tasted this good. Her very breath tasted like the nectar of the gods. He could drink her in and want nothing and no one else forever.

An eternity later, Yun pulled his face away from hers, gasping for breath. "Ava, my Ava," he panted. "I love you so much. More than life itself. Please tell me you want me to kiss you again."

If she refused, he would beg. On his knees, if it would help. He would prostrate himself before her.

Her whole face lit with a shy smile. "Yes."

Thirty

Ava paused to catch her breath after yet another blissful kiss from Yun. Somehow, they'd broken the curse.

Reality intruded on her euphoria. "The curse," she said urgently. "Your brothers…the Emperor…they're still under a spell. We must fetch their wives to break the curse." Even as the words left her lips, her heart sank. She'd seen the other princesses in the garden, and their frightened reactions when any man, let alone their own husbands, entered the garden.

None of the other princes' wives held any feelings resembling love for their husbands. None of the princesses would be capable of breaking the curse. Perhaps a mistress or concubine...Ava's thoughts flashed to her mother, and she had an idea. The Empress. Surely the princes' mother held some love for her children. Perhaps even the Emperor, too.

"The Empress," Ava said. "We must go to her and tell her what has happened. Perhaps she can help."

Yun's arms tightened around her. "Perhaps she can. I shall send a servant with a message to my mother. But as long as my brothers and my father are enslaved to that woman, you are in danger. Her hatred for you burns brighter than any torch. Imagine what she will do to you if she knows you can break her spell. No, you must be kept safe. I will take you to my chambers and guard you myself while we wait for word from my mother."

Yun threw open the door to his chamber, gesturing for Ava to precede him inside. Ava took three steps into the room, then stopped dead. She dropped to her knees. "Empress."

"Mother? What are you doing here?" Yun asked, closing the door.

"He's finally done something so stupid it will cost him his throne," the Empress said, resting her elbow on the ornately carved arm of Yun's favourite chair.

Yun hastened to gather up his papers from the desk in front of her. Even his mother wasn't allowed to read his poetry, it seemed.

Ava's blood ran cold. "Who has, Majesty?"

The Empress sighed. "It's Imperial Highness, not Majesty, but it doesn't matter. Get up, girl. You won't do anyone any good down there on your knees."

Ava summoned her courage. "But you can, M…Imperial Highness. Your husband and your sons are under a terrible curse that only you can break."

"It's too late for that. His witch of a mistress is far ahead of you. Even now, the pleasure gardens are awash with blood. First, she ordered my sons to kill their children. Then, their wives. Now, they are fighting each other to the death for my husband's throne and the dubious pleasure of sharing her bed." The Empress eyed Ava. "You must be a witch, too, that you are immune to the curse."

"I'm not a witch. I only have the gift I inherited from my mother – I can see spells and how to break them. No more." Oh, how Ava wished she was more. A powerful enchantress who could cast spells at will.

"Perhaps it will be enough. Will you use your gift to protect my son, keep him from harm, and ensure him a long life?" the Empress demanded.

Ava glanced at Yun "He is my husband. I am honour bound to care for him as a good wife."

The Empress's gaze seemed to see right through Ava to her very soul. "You also vowed to bear him sons."

By the ancestors, she knew. Ava didn't know how, but the Empress knew they hadn't consummated the marriage.

"I will," Ava said, vowing that she would give herself to Yun that very night. If his lovemaking was anything like his kisses, perhaps she might even enjoy it.

"I hope that's true," the Empress said. "For while my family paints the throne room walls with royal blood, there is an army camped outside the walls. If only my stupid husband had lived to see it, for he was right. An army led by your father, girl."

Ava gasped. So much for the alliance Lagle had been sent here for. While Ava had pleaded for peace, her father had been planning war. Maybe even with Lagle as a pawn in the game. "I didn't know. The Queen told me…"

"The witch queen whose daughter commanded the slaughter of my family?" the Empress demanded.

Ava didn't know what to say, so she merely nodded. "She sent me here as a punishment, to serve Lagle, though I am my father's daughter, too. Lagle was determined to be queen here."

The Empress gave a little snort of laughter, that turned into a cough. "Yet fate has other plans. While my family lies dying in the throne room, an army waits to conquer this palace and all who live here. What will you do about it?"

Yun stepped forward. He bowed his head. "I will lead my father's army to victory. I might be the youngest, but I am still a prince. They know me, and will follow me."

"Don't be daft," the Empress snapped. "By the time the army gets here, the palace will be overrun. You can't lead an army if you're dead. You must flee to the Winter Palace, where you will be able to safely take the throne. Find a way to get him there safely, Princess. You are my son's only hope." She waved at a new chest that sat beside the table. "You will find your things in there. Two of the horses you arrived with are packed and saddled in the stables, waiting for you. Lose no time, Princess. Grandsons can wait until the throne is secure." She grimaced, lifting her hand. It was covered in blood. "Swear on the ancestors you will do everything in your power to protect him."

"Mother, we must find you a healer. Let me send for one," Yun begged, reaching for a bell to summon a servant.

As Ava watched, blood ran down the Empress's side to soak her skirt. She did not have long left.

"I swear by my ancestors and my life, I will save your son," Ava vowed.

The Empress nodded and closed her eyes.

"Mother!" Yun howled, but it was too late. The Empress was gone.

Ava fell to her knees beside the chest, rifling through the clothes until she found the gown Bianca had made for her. It was the finest she had, in the style of her father's court. As she stroked the silk, she began to have an inkling of a plan. It was risky, but it was all she had. If it worked, she could save both herself and Yun from her father's army. But it would only work if she had the courage to carry it out.

With trembling hands, Ava garbed herself

for battle.

Thirty-One

"You look like a barbarian princess," Yun remarked, his voice muffled by his guard helmet as he rode behind Ava. "I've never seen a court dress made to be worn by a lady astride a horse."

"I am a barbarian princess," Ava replied. "And you're supposed to be my bodyguard, so please keep quiet. If my father's army knew you were the Emperor's son, and the commander of the opposing army, they'd slaughter you on the spot."

Yun sounded amused. "My sword isn't just for decoration, Princess. I know how to use it. I might prefer poetry to swordsmanship, but I was a match for any man on the battlefield or in the practice ring."

"There has been enough blood spilled today," Ava whispered, fighting tears. "I won't have you killing anyone else, for there are thousands of them and only one of you. I vowed to save you, and I will, but only if you can keep your sword to yourself!"

Yun chuckled. "Yes, mistress."

Not for the first time, Ava regretted her decision to engage in this crazy scheme. But what other choice did she have, if she wanted to keep Yun alive?

None, Ava told herself, which is why she had to remind herself with every step that if her courage failed, Yun would die and his blood would be on her hands. So fishy thoughts were the uppermost in her mind as she guided her horse through the outskirts of the army camp. Though leaping to the top of a waterfall would be easy compared to her task today.

Row upon row of tents stretched as far as she could see, but they were nothing compared to the number of eyes staring at her as she passed. Her neck ached from forcing herself to hold her head high, when it felt far more natural to duck her head to whatever authority presented itself. Even her husband trailed behind her like a subordinate.

"Halt."

Ava was almost grateful for the order, though she knew it would take an even greater act of courage to start her moving again if she stopped.

Nevertheless, the two armed guards barring her way gave her no choice but to rein in her horse.

"You go no further. No camp followers allowed into the main camp before nightfall and he's not allowed in at all. He's a palace guard."

Ava's horse tossed her head, and her

mistress copied her. "I am Princess Ava, daughter of King Chinggis and wife to the Emperor's son, Prince Yun Bataar. I was sent here by my father to secure a marriage alliance with the Emperor, and now I come on behalf of my father's allies to bring him a message. A message I will only give to my father himself, so either summon him or let me pass." She hoped they didn't hear how much her voice shook. If she had to be any more overbearing to gain entrance to the camp, she wasn't sure how she would manage it.

"Princess Ava? The princess who visited the soldiers' swimming pool?" a voice asked eagerly. "Batu, is that really her?"

A soldier scrambled out of one of the tents to her left. His eyes widened and he dropped to his knees, bowing so low his forehead touched the dust. "Princess Ava! We are honoured."

The other soldiers around looked from one another to the kneeling man before bowing just as low. "Princess."

Ava wet her lips. "Please, I need to see my father."

"At once, Princess." The first man leapt to his feet, and Ava recognised him as the soldier who had returned her to the harem. "If you will follow me."

She glanced at Yun. "My escort will come with me. He is my personal bodyguard, and I go nowhere without him."

"As you wish, Princess."

Batu led her to a tent that was larger than the others, but that was all that distinguished it from the rest of the camp. He gestured for her to wait, before slipping inside.

Ava dismounted, hearing Yun doing the same behind her. A groom appeared to take her horse and Ava allowed the animal to be led to the horse line that held her father's own mounts. Beautiful creatures, all of them, just like Falada had been.

Batu backed out of the tent, and bowed low to the man who stepped into the sun. "Majesty," Batu said.

King Chinggis ignored the soldier, for his gaze was fixed on Ava. "Sumi?" he whispered. "I thought you died. Is it really you?"

Thirty-Two

Ava didn't hesitate. She strode forward with her eyes downcast before prostrating herself before the King. "Father," she said. "I am Sumi's daughter. She died giving birth to me, and I was brought up in the harem with your other wives and daughters."

"You are my daughter?" he asked, sounding bemused. "You look just like her."

"Of course, Father. I am Ava, the princess you sent with the Queen's daughter, Lagle, to marry into the Emperor's family and form an alliance, so that our peoples may live in peace." Ava did her best to keep her voice steady, so he wouldn't recognise the lie.

"The bodies in the throne room tell me there is little peace here," the King remarked.

So he already knew. The Emperor had been right about there being spies in his court.

"The Emperor would not agree to an alliance, though Lagle tried everything to persuade him. She took the only action she felt would please you." Or please the Queen, Ava thought but did not say. "With the Emperor dead, the throne falls to one of his sons. With one of them, an alliance can be made."

"My men tell me the sons are dead, too."

Ava stifled a sob. The Empress had been right. So much death. For all their faults, Yun's family didn't deserve to be slaughtered. Yun least of all. She drew in a deep breath, praying silently that her idea would work. "Not all," she said finally. "One survives, and he is a prince of peace, not war. I come to negotiate on his behalf, and all his people. He wishes to rule what lands he has left, without worrying about war. You have enough enemies, but what of an ally, a neighbouring emperor, who swears never to take up arms against you or yours, so that he might build a refined court the like of which the world has never seen before. A court that your grandsons will inherit."

"My grandsons, eh? Which one did you have in mind?"

She fought to keep her voice from shaking. "Why, the one I carry now. Son to the prince, my husband, who seeks an alliance with you for a lasting peace."

"Some husband this prince is, sending a woman as his envoy. Such a coward should not be emperor of anything, let alone husband to one of my daughters."

"I am no coward, sir," Yun said, his boots crunching as he strode to Ava's side. She could see the dusty toes of them, though she didn't dare raise her head. "I am Prince Yun Bataar, the Emperor's son and heir, and husband to

Princess Ava. She begged to be allowed to speak to you first, and I granted her wish, for she has been a good wife to me. I admit to a certain curiosity about her father. Your reputation as a warrior and a conqueror are well-known, but she spoke so highly of you as a father, a man for whom family is important. I, too, wish to protect my family, what is left of it. She is my family, but so are you, honoured father-in-law." He bowed low. "I do not wish to war with family. If you allow us to reach the Winter Palace, we will set up court there, leaving these lands to you. The lands that remain to me will become a place of culture and learning, and no enemy to you. We will be allies, and I will instruct my sons in peace, not war."

"And what of your daughters?" the King demanded.

"Their mother will instruct them, for women are a great mystery to me. All I know is that it is a rare woman who thinks of war with anything but fear," Yun said.

"You have countrywomen who think differently. One who fancies herself a general," the King grumbled. "Cost me some of my best troops when victory seemed certain. There are witnesses who swear they saw her slay my son, their general."

"Da Ying? If you support me as emperor, I will make sure she retires from the army. I'll find her a good marriage where a husband and children will occupy her for the rest of her days. Consider it a favour to my father-in-law."

Ava's breath caught in her throat. The maids had told her stories about Da Ying, the general's daughter turned general. Though the stories Ava had heard included both a husband and child.

The King laughed. "So you wish to be emperor of half a kingdom with no army? You are a strange man, Prince Yun. I could kill you now where you stand, and take all your lands and people for myself. What is there to stop me?"

Ava couldn't muffle the squeak that came

out of her mouth at this. She felt both her husband and her father's eyes on her.

"Family," Yun said gravely. "Far easier to name your daughter Empress, with me as Emperor by her side, and you will always have allies at your back, leaving you free to conquer other lands wherever you choose."

"We have a bargain," the King announced. "As long as my daughter is Empress, and you do not raise an army against me, you may have the Emperor's throne and the lands that remain."

Ava breathed again. "Thank you, Father."

"My Empress prostrates herself to no one," Yun said, helping her to her feet. "Especially not when she carries the next emperor in her belly."

Ava blushed to hear Yun repeat her lie. Surely he didn't believe…

"Come, Princess. Your father is a busy man, and we have a long way to travel to reach the Winter Palace, with much work to do once we reach it." Yun tugged her arm, pulling her out of her father's tent.

He helped her mount her horse, before leaping onto his own. With his helmet on, he appeared every bit her bodyguard again. "Shall we go, Princess?" he asked.

Not trusting her voice, Ava nodded and nudged her horse into a walk.

Thirty-Three

After an hour's ride, they reached a stream, and Yun called a halt. He dismounted and filled their water skins. He passed Ava's up to her and she drank deeply, gratefully, before thanking him.

"So is there a baby?" Yun asked.

Ava reddened. "No. In the western kingdoms, they tell stories about a virgin who gave birth to a son, but I am not her. I…lied. I am sorry."

He swung back into his saddle. "I'm not.

Your lie won us an alliance."

Ava shook her head. "No, your charmed tongue pleased my father. The alliance is your doing, not mine. I merely bought you safe passage through the camp to my father's command tent."

"You bought me a kingdom that should never have been mine. Truly, you deserve to be its Empress." Yun brought his mount close beside hers and reached out to cup her cheek. "Empress Ava Asuka, the bird who flew from her father's court and will be the jewel of mine. The finest poets will proclaim your virtues, and every dancer in the kingdom will clamour to perform for you. I am honoured to call you my wife."

She raised her gaze to meet his dark eyes, and found she could not look away. "I'm not truly your wife yet," she whispered, before he cut her off with a kiss.

The moment stretched delightfully, until with considerable reluctance, he pulled away. "When we reach the Winter Palace, you will be, I promise."

A shiver of anticipation shook Ava from her head to her toes as she swallowed. "Thank you, my prince."

He laughed and spurred his horse forward. "We should hurry home."

What could she do but follow?

Thirty-Four

High in the mountains, huddled closely together to share the warmth of their tiny campfire, Yun waved at the city in the valley below. "The second largest city in my father's kingdom, crowned by the Winter Palace. This will be your home, my Empress."

Ava still wasn't used to the title. She doubted she ever would be. In her mind, the Empress was an incredibly courageous woman who had used her dying moments to save her son's life. And the traditional crowns of the

Emperor and Empress, which Yun had found in the saddle bags on the first night, were almost too heavy for her to lift, let alone wear.

"I am afraid," Ava admitted. "Afraid that I will never live up to the honour of the title that your mother held."

"You have nothing to be afraid of, my Empress. You are the fish who leaped to the top of the waterfall, and tomorrow, you will become the dragon herself." Yun held up her crown which featured a jewelled dragon and set it upon her head.

Ava removed the heavy gold crown and handed it back to him. "No one can fly with so much metal on their head. I would sink to the bottom of the river wearing such a thing."

Yun laughed softly as he returned the crown to its hiding place. "Tomorrow, you will sink into the Empress's silk bed, and as your Emperor, I will love you until your spirit takes flight once more."

He had said similar things every night, never pushing Ava about her promise to give him a son, and she had been grateful for it in the beginning. Now, she felt her courage build.

"I would like to be loved as a princess first," she said slowly. "Loved by a prince, just like in the stories my sister used to tell me in the women's palace when we were children. A prince who saves her, and loves her, and who will lead her to a life of happiness."

"Here? On the ground, without the silken sheets and soft mattress that a princess deserves?" Yun asked.

It was Ava's turn to laugh. They'd slept on the ground for every night of their journey, wrapped together in a rough blanket to share their warmth. She'd almost forgotten what it felt like to sleep in Yun's bed in the palace.

"Yes. Here, in my husband's arms, on our last night alone together before we become part of the world again. Tonight it will be just us – you and me. I am willing, Yun, more willing than I have ever been." Ava kissed him, untying the lacings at the front of her gown with the practiced skill of a woman who didn't need servants for such a thing any more. She shucked off her shift without a second thought, feeling only the joy of her husband's gaze on her as he devoured her body with his eyes alone before he moved in closer for another kiss. His hands on her bare skin felt heavenly. Ava tensed at the slight sting as he eased inside her, before her only sensation was pleasure. Pleasure at finally being one with her husband, and the spiralling desire he coaxed to greater and greater heights until she screamed for joy to the very stars above.

And when the first rays of dawn touched Ava's aching body, she vowed anew that the child they had created among the stars that night would live to see his parents live a long and happy life together. But first, she would wake Yun and enjoy his lovemaking for another hour before they headed down from the heights to take their places at the head of a new and peaceful kingdom.

About the Author

Demelza Carlton has always loved the ocean, but on her first snorkelling trip she found she was afraid of fish.

She has since swum with sea lions, sharks and sea cucumbers and stood on spray drenched cliffs over a seething sea as a seven-metre cyclonic swell surged in, shattering a shipwreck below.

Demelza now lives in Perth, Western Australia, the shark attack capital of the world.

The *Ocean's Gift* series was her first foray into fiction, followed by her suspense thriller *Nightmares* trilogy. She swears the *Mel Goes to Hell* series ambushed her on a crowded train and wouldn't leave her alone.

Want to know more? You can follow Demelza on Facebook, Twitter, YouTube or her website, Demelza Carlton's Place at:

www.demelzacarlton.com

Books by Demelza Carlton

Ocean's Gift series
Ocean's Gift (#1)
Ocean's Infiltrator (#2)
Ocean's Depths (#3)
Water and Fire

Turbulence and Triumph series
Ocean's Justice (#1)
Ocean's Trial (#2)
Ocean's Triumph (#3)
Ocean's Ride (#4)
Ocean's Cage (#5)
Ocean's Birth (#6)
How To Catch Crabs

Nightmares Trilogy
Nightmares of Caitlin Lockyer (#1)
Necessary Evil of Nathan Miller (#2)
Afterlife of Alana Miller (#3)

Mel Goes to Hell series
Welcome to Hell (#1)
See You in Hell (#2)
Mel Goes to Hell (#3)
To Hell and Back (#4)
The Holiday From Hell (#5)
All Hell Breaks Loose (#6)

Romance Island Resort series
Maid for the Rock Star (#1)
The Rock Star's Email Order Bride (#2)
The Rock Star's Virginity (#3)
The Rock Star and the Billionaire (#4)
The Rock Star Wants A Wife (#5)
The Rock Star's Wedding (#6)
Maid for the South Pole (#7)
Jailbird Bride (#8)

The Complex series
Halcyon
Fishtail

Romance a Medieval Fairytale series

Enchant: Beauty and the Beast Retold
Dance: Cinderella Retold
Fly: Goose Girl Retold
Revel: Twelve Dancing Princesses Retold
Silence: Little Mermaid Retold
Awaken: Sleeping Beauty Retold
Embellish: Brave Little Tailor Retold
Appease: Princess and the Pea Retold
Blow: Three Little Pigs Retold
Return: Hansel and Gretel Retold

Printed in Poland
by Amazon Fulfillment
Poland Sp. z o.o., Wrocław